I'm Haunted

Copyright 2020 by Brandon Rhiness. All rights reserved.

ISBN 978-1-988338-08-8

No part of this book may be used or reproduced in any manner whatsoever without the prior written permission of the author and Higher Universe Inc., except in the case of brief quotations embodied in reviews.

Names, characters, businesses, places, events, locales, and incidents are either the products of the author's imagination or used in a fictitious manner. Any resemblance to actual persons, living or dead, or actual events is purely coincidental.

FRIDAY, NOVEMBER 1, 2019

My name is Genesis Brady. Aside from a brief period in junior high, I've never kept a journal before. (I lost that one in a flood when I lived in Calgary in 2013).

I decided to start keeping a journal now because, well…I think my apartment is haunted. Not only that, but there's lots of bad shit happening in my life and it just seems that writing it down is the right thing to do. A way to collect my thoughts. I'm not sure if anyone will ever read this. It's more for myself than for other people. But maybe I'll share it one day. *Maybe.*

Back to the haunting. I'm not even sure where to begin. I guess it started with the knocking. I live in a high-rise apartment building in Edmonton, Alberta, Canada. There are twenty floors in the building, so lots of apartments. I'm used to some noise from the neighbours, but a couple months back strange knocking began to occur. It was on the roof of my apartment. It went on for an hour. It sounded like someone in the apartment above me was hammering on the floor. So I complained to the front office and they informed me the apartment above me has been vacant for months. So…*freaky.*

My apartment has two bedrooms: mine and another next to it that I just use for storage. I started hearing knocking on the other side of the wall, in the spare bedroom. I'd look in there, but it was empty. Another time there was a knock at my front door and nobody was there.

A couple days ago, I came home and papers I had on the coffee table were strewn around the room even though all the windows were closed.

Before you stop reading, no, I'm not crazy. I don't normally believe in this kind of thing, but I can't explain it. I don't really have any family, except my mom. Her and I aren't close. I don't have a large group of friends either, but even if I did, I wouldn't tell them about what's going on. I don't know what they'd think of me.

I'm a U of A art student. Or at least I was. I finished my second year but decided to take a year off. Partly because my whole life is falling apart. Which makes this haunting shit even worse.

I had a fight with my mom and we haven't talked for a couple weeks. I had a falling out with my friend Blythe and now she's messaging me all the time, threatening me and trash-talking me on social media. So I just decided I couldn't handle school on top of everything. I just need a break to focus on myself. It's like I can't even think straight these days. I don't know what's wrong with me. Everything's going to shit.

That's what the fight with my mom was about. She was livid when I told her I wasn't going back to school. Well, guess what, Mom? I make my own decisions now.

I live with my dog, Poe. He's an 11-year-old pug. He's so ugly he's cute.

Ok, right after I wrote that last line, I heard my door creak and turned around to see it closing on its own. Just a little bit. But since no windows in my apartment are open,

I don't see how it could move. What do you do in a situation like this? I used to like horror movies. It's totally different when it's happening to you.

Is it a ghost? Why would it appear all of a sudden? I don't know anybody who died recently. My dad died, but that was when I was 12. I'm 20 now.

Whoa. My door just opened all the way on its own. I wasn't expecting things to happen live as I'm writing. It's exhilarating on top of being scary. My heart is racing. I don't think it can hurt me, but I just don't like it. I'm starting to have trouble sleeping. But it hasn't done anything to me in the middle of the night. Yet, at least.

I have a best friend named Dan. I met him the first week of my first year at school. We never dated or anything, we're just friends. But we're really close. He's the best. I haven't told him about the weird stuff going on because I don't know how he'll take it and the last thing I need now is to lose another friend.

Since this whole thing started, I've been readings lots about other people's experiences with hauntings on the internet. I've chatted with people too and some of them have interesting stories. So I might include some of their stories in this journal, just because they're interesting.

For example, I was talking with a young woman from Florida named Margaret. She says it's usually some sort of event that triggers the whole thing. And sometimes it takes another event to stop it. It doesn't have to be anything major, or anything paranormal. For example, she said the landlord did some renovations to the house she was renting and right after that, weird stuff started happening. Objects being moved around, etc. It went on for a few weeks and she was thinking of moving, but then her cousin moved in with her and it all stopped. That's interesting. Maybe my situation will only last a few weeks.

Of course, I've read about other people whose hauntings have gone on for years no matter what they tried.

SATURDAY, NOVEMBER 2, 2019

Today is horrible! Poe ran away!

Last night, he started acting weird. He was growling at something in the kitchen that wasn't there, which was really freaking me out. Then he laid down and went to sleep. But this morning, he wouldn't wake up. I shook him, but he wouldn't wake up. I carried him to the car to drive him to the vet.

We were half-way there when all of a sudden, he wakes up in the back seat, his usual self again. So I turned around and went home. When I opened the door he jumped out of the car and ran off!

He ran across 122 street and I nearly got hit by a car chasing him. Stupid traffic slowed me down. I probably could have caught him but he ran around behind some apartment building and I couldn't find him. I looked everywhere. Some guy asked what I was doing and helped me look, but we couldn't find him. So I don't know what to do. I'm literally crying as I write this.

I just drove around the neighbourhood again looking for Poe but couldn't find him. He has his dog tags, so someone's bound to find him and return him, right? I'm just worried he'll get hit by a car. Or he'll run into the River Valley and get eaten by some animal. But I can't think like that. I'm sure he'll turn up. Then I'll give him a big hug and never let him out of my sight again. This is awful.

I posted a picture of him on Facebook and said he was missing. I asked all my Edmonton friends to share it.

I'm really worried. Poe keeps me company so I didn't feel alone. If I have to live in a haunted apartment all by myself, I don't know how I'll survive.

SUNDAY, NOVEMBER 3, 2019

It's been twenty-four hours and no sign of Poe. I'm so beyond worried. I went down to the campground in the River Valley and asked if I could put up a poster in the lobby of the main building. The girl there said she'd ask her manager. Hopefully they'll put it up. I don't see why they wouldn't.

I went to all the apartment buildings in the area and taped up posters on their front doors. Somebody has to see something. I just really hope Poe is ok. What's that rule?

If someone isn't found in the first 48 hours they won't be found? Does that apply to dogs too? Poor Poe is out there hungry and alone.

I was watching TV tonight and it felt like someone else was in the room! I've heard people talk about the feeling of being watched and never knew what they meant. Now I know. It's scary as fuck. It was like someone was standing at the edge of the couch, staring at me. I could feel them there, like a presence, but couldn't see them.

I don't know what I should do. Maybe it's just all in my head because of everything going on. Why does everything in my life go wrong at the same time?!

I just went for a walk to look for Poe (and clear my head). I came home and the curtains in the living room were blowing around wildly. The wind outside was howling, which was weird because it wasn't windy two minutes earlier when I came back from my walk. But I am on the 13th floor so sometimes it gets windier up here. Many times the windows rattle with the force of the wind. I've gotten used to it. But with everything else happening, anything the slightest bit odd or creepy is magnified by a hundred. And I don't remember leaving the window open. I always close the windows when I leave because one time I left my bedroom window open and it rained. It got in all over my laptop and ruined it. I'll never make that mistake again.

But, like so many other things, I can't be totally certain I closed the windows. So there's always that doubt.

About the whole 13th floor thing - I'm sure anyone who reads this will make a big deal about it but I don't think it has anything to do with what's going on. I've lived here for two years with no problems. So it's not the floor number. That's just a superstition. When I moved in, I had the choice between an apartment on floor 19 and 13. I would have rather lived higher up, but the one on the 13th floor had these cool shelving units in the hallway that leads from the front door to the living room.

MONDAY, NOVEMBER 4, 2019

Not to get all existential, but it seems like there's a black cloud hanging over my life lately. Not because of the haunting. Separate from that. I don't know how to explain it. It's like there's no longer a light at the end of the tunnel.

I don't know if I'm depressed or what. I've never seen a psychiatrist or counselor or whatever before. I don't know if I should. It's probably expensive and I can't afford it. I'm not suicidal or anything like that. But I used to always be a bright, happy person. Now I'm not.

I'm starting to think about darker things too. Some things that I don't even want to write because they're so twisted. I don't think it's too big of a deal. I mean people watch horror movies and that doesn't mean they're going to do anything bad.

Thoughts can't hurt you. It's just something I noticed and since I'm trying to be completely honest in this journal, I thought I'd mention it.

It's November so it's probably going to snow any day now. I wish all of this could have happened in the summer. It would be easier to deal with. Haunting plus life falling apart plus winter is a bad combination.

The strange knockings keep happening sporadically. It's possible they're all from people in other apartments, but I don't think so. There's a lot of opening and closing of doors, too. Mainly my bedroom door and my sliding closet door. It usually happens when I'm not in the room. I'll come back to find the door open when I was sure I left it closed, or vice versa. Sometimes I see it happen which always sends a chill up my spine.

I'm starting to think I overreacted yesterday thinking there was someone watching me. Maybe it was just nerves because of the whole thing with Poe. I'm not sure.

There's still no word on Poe. My Facebook post has been shared 30 times as of now. People are giving me all sorts of sympathy in their comments, but that doesn't help find Poe. Get your lazy asses out there and help me look for him! Not that I don't appreciate it. It's not their problem. I don't know what I'd say in a situation like that. You never know what another person is going through.

I miss school. I miss being around people. I rarely go out anymore. I don't hang out with Blythe anymore so other than Dan, I have no meaningful human contact. It's kind of sad. I can see when I'm 80 and all my friends are dead, living alone with my dog. But it's not supposed to happen *now*. It's really sad. But feeling sorry for myself isn't going to get me anywhere, so I should probably stop and think happy thoughts. *Think happy thoughts…think happy thoughts …think happy thoughts…* (In case you're wondering, I'm making a big, stupid, happy face right now. Lol. Yeah, I know. I'm totally lame.)

I was just lying on the couch, texting with Dan, when I heard noise in the spare bedroom. It sounded like someone rooting through the boxes in there. I went in and flicked on the light. Of course I didn't see anything and the noise stopped. I could almost feel a presence in there, but it wasn't as strong as I felt the other day. And I'm not even sure *that* one was real, so it's really hard to know what to believe.

That's the thing with "sixth sense" perception. With other senses, you grow to trust them over the course of your life. If you see something, you believe it. You *saw* it. End of question. But with having a feeling…it's hard to prove. Just because you're creeped out doesn't mean you're right. I've met guys I was totally creeped out by when I first met them who turn out to be really great people. On the flip-side, I've met guys I trusted who turned out to be creeps. Point being I'm not sure if there is a presence in the house or if I just sense it because I'm scared.

Speaking of creepy guys, when I first met Dan, he approached me at a bar and started talking to me. My first thought was, "Great, another guy hitting on me." But he wasn't and he turned out to be the *least* creepy, most awesome guy I've ever met.

It's weird holding a normal conversation with Dan with this stuff going on. I want to tell him what's happening so bad. I just can't risk losing him as a friend. He's a cool guy and I love him to death, but he doesn't believe in any of this stuff. We used to watch those ghost-hunting shows on TV and Dan would just make fun of them. Anything like that – bigfoot, aliens, he just thinks is stupid. So if I told him what was happening, he wouldn't believe me and he'd make fun of me. It would probably lead to a fight and drive a wedge between us. So it's best to keep quiet and pretend everything's cool.

Blythe would believe me. She's into this kind of stuff. She thinks she's some kind of witch now. She got into witchcraft about a year ago and then it was all she talked about. She tried to get me involved, but I had no interest. It's really stupid if you ask me. She was like, "It's not what you think it is, Genesis. Movies make witchcraft look evil, but it's actually about being one with the Earth." That's not exactly what she said, but it was some sort of stupid shit like that.

She actually took me to a séance a few months back. It was so stupid. Not to mention boring. She was right about one thing - it's not like you see in the movies. It was with these new friends she found. They were all weirdos. Self-proclaimed psychics and people who never grew out of their goth phase from high school. I didn't fit in, but I promised Blythe I'd try it once. It was at some guy's house in Castle Downs. There were seven of us. We sat around a table and held hands and the guy whose house it was pretended he was "channeling" dead people. One, he said, was a relative of his and another was some random spirit he said was in him. People asked him questions and he answered like he was the spirit, but it was obviously *him* answering. He was only giving one or two-word answers, so it's not like he put a lot of thought into it. Idiot.

Everyone acted so amazed because he had answers to their questions. But he could make up anything he wanted because there was no way to confirm the answers. One of the girls asked the name of her future husband. He was like, "Lucas," and she was like, "Oh, my God! That's amazing!" He could have said *anything*! It was so dumb. Even Blythe rolled her eyes at me a couple times. When it was my turn to ask a question, I didn't ask something that couldn't be proven, I asked what my dad's name was. Of course, the idiot got it wrong. He said "Larry." (Just in case you're wondering, my dad's name was William).

After that we just sat around drinking. That was more fun than the séance. I left when they all decided to do mushrooms. Blythe stayed behind. Either way, I'd rather not hang out with those people again. If Blythe finds their company better than mine, she's more than welcome to be part of their little group.

MICHELLE'S STORY

I thought I'd share another story from someone I met online. Her name is Michelle. I don't have a lot of real friends, so I spend a lot of time talking to people on the internet to ward off loneliness and boredom. It only partially works.

Anyways, Michelle seems really cool. She's from Saskatchewan. Most of the stories I've heard (and movies I've seen) always have poltergeist-type stuff happening first, then people get possessed after it escalates. But in Michelle's case, it seemed to go straight to possession. Not her, but her roommate.

Michelle is the same age as me and she was living with a friend from University named Dani. One day Dani started acting "fucked-up," as Michelle put it. She would just sit there, staring, like she was in a waking coma. Michelle would wave her hand in front of Dani's face and shake her. Eventually she'd snap out of it with no recollection of what happened.

After a while, she started having false memories. She'd talk about things her and Michelle supposedly did together, but they never actually happened. One of them was being on a cruise together. Michelle said she'd never been on a cruise in her life, and neither had Dani as far as she knew.

Her stories started getting more "out there." One of them was being on the run from the police. Another was fighting the Japanese, like a war story. Michelle told Dani she needed to see a doctor, but Dani insisted she was fine.

She eventually started referring to herself in the third person. The next step was Dani referring to herself as "Big Man Carl" (wtf?). She'd talk and act like a man and say demeaning stuff about "Dani." Dani's voice started changing, sounding more like a man. Even her facial features started to change. "Big Man Carl" would talk about working in the coal mines and how his "bitch of a wife" didn't appreciate him.

It got to the point where Michelle was so scared that she just moved out one day without telling Dani (or her new personality). This happened a year ago and she hasn't seen Dani since. That's pretty freaky.

I know it sounds silly, but I'm kind of worried about getting possessed. I don't really believe in it (despite Michelle's story). I think Dani had mental issues. But I've read other stories about possession that make me wonder. I've also read that you can't just become possessed out of the blue. You have to participate in some way and "invite it in." Which I have no intention of doing, so I should be fine. I've just read a lot about the escalations of hauntings. It starts with simple poltergeist-type stuff, like I'm going through, then gets more intense until an entity takes over your body. Ok, just talking about this is freaking me out. I'm going to go for a walk.

I was out walking and it started raining. I tried to catch a bus, but just missed it. I just got home and I'm soaked to the bone. It looks like I jumped in a swimming pool with my clothes on. Some guy in the lobby gave me a weird look.

TUESDAY, NOVEMBER 5, 2019

There's good news and bad news. The good news is the haunting stuff seems to be tapering off. Nothing much has happened in the last couple days. Or maybe I've been overreacting about something that wasn't there since the beginning. Stuff like this makes you doubt your sanity. "Did I actually see (or hear) what I thought I did?" You start doubting your memories. And you justify it to yourself. "It's not that bad." When really, *it is*. Whatever. I hope it's going away for good.

I wonder if a lot of people in mental institutions are there because of paranormal stuff. I wouldn't doubt it. I mean, who do your turn to? If you're sick, you go to a doctor. If you're not well mentally, you see a psychiatrist. But with hauntings, who do you go to? Those stupid ghost hunters? A psychic? If you told a psychiatrist about this stuff, they'd assume you're lying or hallucinating. Most people don't believe it's real. Neither do I, 100%. I still think what's going on here is explainable.

I really don't know what to think. I just know the whole situation is fucking with my mind and I wish it would stop. Sometimes, quite a while will go by with nothing happening and I'll think, "maybe it's over." Then it will happen again and I'm back to square one. That's why I don't want to get my hopes up now.

I wish I could move. I'd just have to come up with the damage deposit for a new place, which I don't know if I could do. I didn't get my student loan money this year because I'm not in school, so money is tight. My mom's been helping me out but now that we're fighting, I can't exactly ask her for money.

The bad news is Poe still hasn't been found. I went to the police station today but they said there's nothing they can do. It's not really a "police matter." I hate dealing with the police. Even when I haven't done anything wrong, it just seems like they're out to get me. I'm always nervous around them. When there's one behind me when I'm driving, I'm always sweating, gripping the steering wheel like they're going to haul me off to jail. I don't know why. I've never been in trouble with the law before. Except for one speeding ticket. When I got pulled over, I almost started crying. The cop was like, "Don't worry, it's ok. It's only a ticket. Just slow it down." He was pretty nice, but the guy I dealt with today was such a jerk. I could tell he couldn't care less about my dog. He could have at least *pretended* like he cared.

I went to a bunch of dog shelters in the city, like the Humane Society and stuff. They were more helpful. At least they cared. They took down Poe's information and his picture and said they'd let me know if he shows up. It's obvious they love animals.

I'm forcing myself to come to terms with the fact that Poe might not be coming back. In all likelihood he's dead. I hate to think the worst, but it might help ease the shock when I find out. Or maybe I'll never find out. Maybe he'll never come back. Maybe some nice family took him in and he's happy out there somewhere. Yeah…that's what I'll force myself to think. (cough …delusional…cough).

I saw Blythe in my neighbourhood today. I stopped for gas at the gas station across the street and I saw her in the store. I don't think she saw me. I wonder if she's spying on me. She's stopped texting me twenty times a day and calling me in the middle of the night. I told her I'd go to the cops if she did it again. If I see her near my building, I will call the cops.

I can't believe she turned into this whole other person. We've been friends since grade 10 and all of a sudden, she hates me. The whole thing was so stupid. We'd been drifting apart ever since she started hanging around weird people and doing that witchcraft nonsense. But she started dating this guy named Mike. And if you saw him and you saw her, you'd be like, "How the hell are they together?" Mike is such a sweet, innocent (ok, I'll say it, "dumb") guy. Blythe is my friend and all but she's not always the nicest person. She tends to use people and spit them out. She was different with me, that's why we were friends. I've seen her do it to guys before, but with Mike it was different. He's such a sweetheart. He doesn't deserve to have her treat him like that.

Anyways, I basically told her that she was using him and she should break up with him and let him down easy. She didn't take that very well. She got super pissed off, accusing me of wanting to break them up because I wanted Mike for myself. Which is absolutely not the case.

Then she called me in the middle of the night one time, yelling at me, saying the reason I don't want her to have a boyfriend is I'm a lesbian and I'm in love with her. Not true either. And I don't care if she has a boyfriend, she's dated a ton of guys since we met, I just don't want anyone's feelings to get hurt. But she was like, "As if I'd ever date you, you dyke bitch!" and all this other stuff. I think she was drunk. She sounded like a crazy person. I hung up and she kept trying to call me back.

She even called Dan, trash-talking me. He told her to fuck off and hung up. Lol. Dan doesn't put up with bullshit like that. Neither should I.

Anyways, I was at West Edmonton Mall one time and I ran into Mike. We ate in the food court and talked for a bit. I didn't say anything to him about Blythe. We just talked about school and art or whatever. Somehow Blythe found out that Mike and I were together and fucking lost it on me even worse.

She sent me all these messages threatening to beat me up. She started posting all this horrible stuff on social media. She didn't mention me by name but it would be obvious to anyone who knows us who she was talking about. I ended up having to block her.

I'm glad she's not messaging me anymore, but it makes me nervous seeing her across the street from where I live. Maybe it was a coincidence that she happened to be there. I just don't want her bothering me anymore.

I guess the good that came of it is that her and Mike broke up. Apparently, she accused him of cheating on her with me and he finally grew some balls and dumped her. I don't want that kind of drama in my life. Of course with the haunting going on during all that, it was almost too much to bear.

I'm starting to wonder if I should call my mom. I just can't tell her what's happening because she'd probably have me locked away.

From reading all this you might assume my life is always chaotic melodrama, but it's not. This is all very rare. My life is usually boring.

They found Poe! He's dead! Someone stabbed him to death! It better not have been Blythe or I'll fucking kill her!

WEDNESDAY, NOVEMBER 6, 2019

I'm still trying to process what happened to Poe. Dan came over last night after I got the news. He comforted me and slept on the couch just so I'd have someone here. He's the best friend I've ever had.

A police officer came over to give me the news and ask some questions. I guess now that it's a case of animal cruelty, they care. At least this cop was nice. He was younger and actually seemed like he'd be a cool person if the circumstances were different. He was understanding and nice about the whole thing.

They found Poe in the bushes along a path in the River Valley not too far from here. Some guy was walking his dog and the dog started sniffing at something and the guy looks and there's poor Poe, stabbed a whole bunch of times. I could tell the cop didn't want to tell me the details because he didn't want to upset me, but he told me anyways. I had to know.

Who does that to a dog?

He asked if I had enemies. It totally sounded like a movie line, but that's exactly what he said: "Do you have any enemies?" Of course the first thing I said was, "Blythe." He said they'd look into it. I don't know if it was her or not. Honestly, I can't bring myself to believe it was. Not even Blythe can be that psycho. I think. It was probably some random disturbed person, destined to be a serial killer. Or maybe he already is.

What if Blythe is a serial killer?

Ok, maybe that's going to far.

Maybe I'm just thinking crazy shit to overcompensate for what happened to Poe. I'm actually quite traumatized by it. Why did it have to happen now with everything else going on?

Remember what I said about the black cloud over my life?

I think the "presence" is back. The whole night it's felt like someone has been following me. You know how you can sense when someone is standing right behind you? It was like that. The whole night. Wherever I went in the apartment. Every room. Even the bathroom. I'd turn around and reach out with my arm, but I couldn't feel anything. It might be the worst thing that's happened yet. The other day it felt like someone was standing by the couch, now it's moving and following me around.

I left the apartment for a bit and when I came back it wasn't there anymore, but I was still scared. I called Dan to see if he could come over again. He only stayed for an hour because he had a birthday party to go to. I couldn't tell him why I wanted him there because I don't want him to think I'm weird. So I just said I was still upset over Poe and needed a friend. Which is true, I guess.

It kind of makes me jealous that Dan is still in school and has a social life. I miss that part of school so much. It's not like I partied all the time, but it was nice just to be around people.

Dan and I have a weird friendship. Most of the time we hang out it's just the two of us. It's not like we have mutual friends and we all hang out together. He has his friends and I have (had) mine. But we also have each other. Nothing wrong with it, I guess, it's just strange.

Blythe met Dan a couple times but they didn't really talk much. Even though I've known Blythe way longer, I still considered Dan my best friend. Before he came along, I'd refer to Blythe as my best friend just because she was the one I spent the most time with, but she never felt like a best friend. More like some person I hung around with all the time. And when I met Dan it was like, "Move over Blythe, Dan's my best friend now." Of course I never told her that.

My best friend before Blythe was Corinne, but she died in grade 9. She had a weak heart and I guess it just gave out. She fell down during track and field. The ambulance came and took her to the hospital but she died soon after. I wasn't even at school that day. I was home sick (actually, I was faking it). It's weird to think about that now. A 14-year-old girl dying of a heart attack. I wonder if Corinne and I would still be friends in she was alive.

I watched Dan tonight to see if there was any sign he was picking up on the paranormal stuff but he seemed normal. Of course there was no knocking or any of that. I wish there was and he heard it. It might be an opening to lead into a discussion about what's happening. And it would be proof I wasn't making it up. But no such luck.

I'm scared to go to sleep. What if something is in my room? But I have to sleep. What if it is all in my head? It'll only get worse if I'm sleep-deprived. The last thing I need is to further blur the line between fantasy and reality.

I'm going to take a sleeping pill. My mom left some when she came to visit. She lives in Thunder Bay, Ontario. I don't even see how my mom needs sleeping pills seeing how much she drinks every night.

She moved out there pretty much right after I turned 18. I got my own place near the University when I started school, then a few weeks later she's like, "I'm moving to Thunder Bay." That was kind of random. We have no family there and she didn't know anyone there. Apparently, she just read somewhere that it's a nice place to live and up and moved.

It's not like I need her to take care of me; I'm a grown adult, but I am an only child and dad's gone, so I don't see why she couldn't stay here. I can't shake this subtle feeling that she was just waiting to ditch me the second she could.

We Skype occasionally, but we're not close. It's probably better this way. It's not like she was the best mother in the world. But that's a story for another time.

Oh, yeah, the sleeping pills. She left some here when she came to visit last Christmas. I take them once in a while if I'm having trouble sleeping. I'll go take one, then sleep with the light on. I'll update in the morning if anything happens.

THURSDAY, NOVEMBER 7, 2019

First order of business - it's like a million degrees in this apartment. Something must be wrong with the heat. I'll go tell the front office about it. For being so high up, this apartment is surprisingly nice in the summer. It doesn't get too hot. When we lived in Calgary, we were on the 3rd floor and it was sweltering in the summer. However, it is November now, so there's no reason I should have sweat soaking through my shirt.

The sleeping pill worked. I was out like a light. However, when I woke up this morning, my bedroom light was off. I distinctly left it on. But it's possible I turned it off in the middle of the night. I can't remember. Sometimes I get up in the night to go to the bathroom and I'm only half-conscious. It's possible I got up and flicked the light off on my way back out of sheer habit. But part of me knows I'm just making excuses. The light turned off on its own. Or something turned it off. I know it.

The police talked to Blythe about Poe's death and now she's pissed. She sent me this long, rambling email berating me about it. She called me a stupid bitch and said she could stab me, but she'd never hurt a dog. I can deal with that. She's said worse to me. (And smart move, Blythe. Threaten to stab someone when you're already under suspicion from the police). But what really freaked me out is the last line of her email: "Hope you're sleeping well at night."

What the hell does that mean? Does she know what's going on here? I don't see how she could. Maybe it's a coincidence. Maybe she means I should have trouble sleeping because of guilt over what I did to her or some stupid thing like that. Ugh, who knows. I'm trying to let her abuse just roll off me. She's not part of my life anymore and I'm not going to respond to her.

However, something tells me she's not the one who killed Poe. Blythe is a lot of things, but she's not that evil. She wouldn't hurt an animal. And she's right – I could see her killing me before killing a dog.

Anyways, I'm going to go cook some pasta.

This is unexpected. I just got a text from Blythe apologizing for everything. That's a first. It was around 11:00am when she sent those threats, now it's 7:00pm and she's retracting everything. You can understand my scepticism.

But here's the freaky thing. This is word for word what she just texted me: "I wish I could stop what's happening, but I can't."

What the hell?!!

Is she talking about the haunting? That's not possible. It started after we had our fight. I haven't spoken with her since. At first, I responded to her abusive messages, but I certainly never mentioned anything about the ghost. I've never told a soul about it. There's no way she could have read this journal because it's on my laptop, which is password protected. I haven't shared it publicly. This is really tripping me out.

I have been chatting with people online about my experiences, but I've never posted publicly. Blythe isn't part of any of those paranormal Facebook groups (I checked). So I doubt anyone I talked with could have told her.

I want to message her back and ask what she's talking about, but it will just lead to a fight. I know it.

I can't help thinking she's somehow responsible for all this. She's into that witchcraft stuff. Did she put a curse on me? Or did one of those losers she hangs out with? I'm not sure what I believe anymore. I never believed in ghosts and haunted houses before, but that's starting to change. What else could I be wrong about?

The knocking started up again. And there was a scratching sound, like a dog trying to claw its way through the wall. It started on one side of the room, went up the wall, across the roof, then down the wall right behind me. I got up and started walking away, trying to get away from it, but it seemed to follow me, first into my room then down the hall to the front door. I yelled, "Fuck off!" and it stopped. Is it Poe's ghost or something?

That's the paranormal update. As for my bullshit life update, I'm out of money and need a job. I sent resumes to a bunch of places. Normally I'd ask my mom to borrow money, but that isn't an option. Plus, I need something to do during the day. I feel like I'm going crazy stuck here. I want to get out of this place as soon as possible and move somewhere that isn't haunted. I'd give anything to resume a normal life.

I haven't talked to Dan in a few days. I should see what he's up to.

Here's something new. I went for a walk. There's a bike path that goes from 122 street to Southgate. It's nice so I walk down it quite a bit. This time, there was a guy walking his dog coming towards me. The dog seemed normal until it got close, then it just started viciously growling and barking at me for no reason. It scared the shit out of me. I had to walk into the bushes just to get away from it. The guy apologized and pulled the dog away. I continued on but looked back and the dog was fine. Some kids walked by and dog ignored them. It was something about *me*.

That freaked me out. I kept walking and as I got closer to Southgate a dog in someone's back yard started growling at me! And when I say these dogs were "barking and growling," I mean it's on a level I've never seen before. Everyone's had dogs bark at them. But never like this. It was like they had rabies or something. The one in the yard kept jumping like it was trying to get over the fence. I was worried he'd make it, so I ran.

When I got to the intersection near the mall, I had to wait at a traffic light. There's

an LRT crossing there so sometimes you have to wait forever for the light to turn.

While I was waiting, a truck pulled up to the stoplight and there was a dog in the back

seat. It started freaking out on me too! Savage barking. The window was rolled down

a bit and I thought the dog was going to break it and jump out. The guy driving

yanked the dog back by the collar and rolled the window up. He looked at me, likely

wondering what his dog was barking at.

What is happening?! I went into the mall and got a coffee, which didn't help calm

my nerves. My heart was beating a mile a minute. I walked around the mall until I

calmed down, then I walked home. I went down 51st Ave (the main street) instead of

going back down the bike path. Half-way home I saw a couple with a dog coming

towards me. I nearly had a panic attack but the dog just walked by, barely noticing

me.

I'm disturbed by the whole thing. It might not have bothered me so much if it

wasn't for Poe and the whole haunting. That all just gives it a creepier edge.

Nothing else happened the rest of the night. I heard a few knocks and weird noises

but nothing out of the ordinary. (Funny that ghostly knocks and noises have become

"ordinary" and barely scare me anymore). I don't know if that's good or bad. The doors haven't been moving lately, which is a relief. I find the physical moving of objects scarier than the noises. But I could really do without any of it.

FRIDAY, NOVEMBER 8, 2019

I'll remember today for the rest of my life. I felt pretty good when I got up in the morning. Aside from the bathroom door being closed when I went to shower in the morning, which is unusual (but not necessarily paranormal), the whole day was incident free.

I did laundry and replied to emails and messages I've been neglecting. It felt like I was getting my life back under control. I started cooking dinner. By "cooking" I mean putting a store-bought frozen lasagna in the oven.

The first inkling I had that something was wrong was when this *stillness* came over the room. It's like the energy changed. The best way I can describe it is that I could feel electricity in the room. It got quiet, even though it was already quiet. It's hard to explain. I could feel pressure in my ears, like when your ears pop on an airplane. Like the pressure in the room was changing.

Nothing was happening, but I felt creeped out. You know that feeling when the hair on the back of your neck stands up? It felt *wrong*.

I started making a salad and all of a sudden, I felt that same presence I did before, like someone standing in the room. I was totally freaked out, but I couldn't see anyone. I carried on making supper, but I was on edge.

I was pouring a glass of water when a voice coming from the living room said, "No!" It was loud and clear. I hope nobody reading this ever hears anything like it because it curdled my blood. It was the most terrifying thing I've ever heard. I never want to experience anything like that again. It was such a horrifying voice. I couldn't tell if it was male or female, it was like something in between, but had a child-like quality to it. But it was deep. It's so hard to explain. Let's just say it wasn't human. It was like something imitating a human and getting it close, but not quite.

It was scary enough to send me running from the apartment, into the street, sans shoes and coat. Not ideal for November in Canada.

I just now (after being outside far too long) worked up the courage to come back up to my apartment. I'm so paranoid I'm going to hear that voice again. I keep looking over my shoulder as I'm typing this, like something's standing behind me. I'm so scared.

I'm also an idiot. I forgot about my lasagna in the oven. I lost my appetite and wasn't thinking about food. When I finally realized I left it in there, it was burned to shit. I opened the oven and smoke came billowing out. It set off the smoke detector with its ear-piercing, loud wail. It's enough to make your head explode.

Of course, this is a high-rise building with hundreds of people in it, so everyone had to evacuate. I felt like such an idiot because it was totally my fault. There were shitloads of people congregated in the lobby and outside the building. The fire department sent four trucks. Total overkill since there's no fire, but I guess they didn't know that. I was going to call and tell them it's a false alarm, but before I could, I heard sirens and saw them coming up the street. When they arrived, I told them what happened, but they had to go up and check anyways. I've never been so embarrassed. They finally turned the alarm in the building off and left. Of course there were like 300 people waiting to get back up to their apartments and the elevators only hold so many. There are two elevators, but it still would have taken forever, so I walked up to the 13th floor.

Turns out I'm not in as good of shape as I used to be. The stairs nearly killed me. I stopped a couple times to catch my breath. Each floor had a different smell. Weird. Also, the 8th floor has brand new carpets in the hall. What makes them so special?

It still smells like smoke in my apartment. I'm so stupid! At least all the excitement helped distract me from what happened earlier.

How am I supposed to sleep here now that this fucking thing is talking to me? I texted Dan and asked him to come over.

SATURDAY, NOVEMBER 9, 2019

Dan didn't text me back yet, which is weird. For the lazy guy he can be sometimes, he's actually really good responding to messages. Usually within the hour. But it is Saturday morning. Maybe he was out last night and he's sleeping in, hungover. Normally I wouldn't think anything of it, but after all the surreal shit happening to me, I'm scrutinizing everything.

I was too scared to stay in the apartment last night, so I left and walked around the city for a few hours. I passed a couple dogs and they didn't bark.

I finally came home and sat on the couch all night, watching TV, half-expecting to hear that voice again, but I didn't. Of course now I'm starting to think, "Did I really hear a voice?" I know damn-right well I did, but I think the human brain goes to great lengths in deceiving itself so it doesn't have to change its long-held, basic beliefs. Such as, "Voices can't just come out of thin air." But I heard that voice. No doubt about it.

Skeptics will say it could have come from outside or the apartment next door. But no. I know the difference between a voice thirteen floors down on the street and one ten feet away, in my own living room.

Being awake all night, dreading hearing that voice again, was harder to deal with than actually hearing it. Just the thought that it could happen at any moment. I've calmed down a bit, but I'm still scared to sleep here.

I messaged my friend Melinda to see if I could stay with her tonight. She said that's no problem. I told her they're spraying my building for roaches and I can't be here for twenty-four hours. They actually sprayed my apartment for roaches last year. They sprayed the whole building. I saw a few in my apartment. They're gross as hell. But I talked to Mrs. Pearson, who lives up the hall and she said some people had hundreds in their suites. Imagine that. I'd almost rather have the ghost. It was only six hours that you couldn't be in your apartment after they sprayed, but I doubt Melinda will look that up and blow my story.

It's kind of awkward because I haven't spoken to Melinda in over a year. I met her a few years ago when we worked at Kato's together. We hung out a bit outside work but drifted apart. We're still on good terms, but you know how it is. Life gets in the way and you just don't see people as much. It was my fault. She invited me out but I'd always say no. Nothing against her. I just didn't feel like it at the time. She eventually stopped asking. I felt bad and I always meant to reach out to her to see what's up, but I never did. Of course the more time passes, the easier it is not to do it. Now I need something, so I contacted her. That makes me feel great! (That was sarcasm if it didn't translate through the page).

I just got home from Melinda's. I feel well-rested. It was cool to catch up with her, but I didn't tell her what's going on. I did tell her about Poe. We had fun staying up talking and laughing. It actually felt like I had a normal life for a while.

She's still working at Kato's. I haven't been in touch with anyone else from there since I quit. But apparently this one guy there, Shawn, proposed to her! They weren't even dating. They'd never even hung out together outside work. And he went out, bought a ring, got down on one knee and proposed! At work! Of course she said no. She told the boss and Shawn got fired. Apparently, he came back wanting to talk to her but they threatened to call the cops and he left.

Shawn always creeped me out. He was so weird. Sometimes he'd come talk to me when I was eating lunch and he'd sit way too close and talk too much. I'd have to say, "Shawn, can you leave me alone, please?" He'd apologize and leave, but he'd do it again a few days later. He wasn't the reason I quit, but he was one of the reasons. I feel bad that Melinda had to go through that. Why do people do things like that?

Dan still hasn't texted me back. I messaged him again because maybe he forgot, but he's not replying. That's totally not like him. I'm kind of worried. Maybe I'm being over-protective.

I have to say I feel totally alone. I can't tell anyone I know what's happening because that might alienate people even more. I've been reading about hauntings and

other paranormal stuff on the internet and reading peoples' stories, but it doesn't help.
I know it sounds cruel, but I still don't believe a lot of them. That might sound weird
since it's happening to *me*, but instead of finding comfort in hearing other people
have gone through similar things, I find myself feeling more distanced. I don't know
if they're telling the truth or not. And so many of them seem strange. Sometimes I
just like chatting with these people I meet online as a means of distraction. It keeps
my mind off my own problems. A temporary solution.

It doesn't help that all those stupid ghost-hunting shows on TV made a complete
mockery of the whole thing. *Yeah*, I'm going to invite a bunch of losers with no lives
into the house to run around in the dark with night-vision on, making a huge deal
about the slightest sound they hear, yet proving nothing. (Exhale! Lol. Sorry about the
rant).

I don't want to hire a psychic either. They're full of shit too. But maybe I could
find one of those paranormal investigators. A reputable one. I've heard some bigger
cities have a "paranormal society." If I get someone like that instead of a TV amateur,
maybe they could help. If they deal with stuff like this all the time it won't be as
embarrassing.

On a side note, I can't imagine why someone going through this would ever want
to be on TV to discuss it. I find it kind of embarrassing. It's like having some disease.
Like, "Why did this happen to me?"

I'm thinking about contacting my mom just for someone to talk to. Even if she's annoying, at least she's temporary company. Maybe not the nicest thing to say about your own mother, but she brought it on herself.

EDDIE'S STORY

Eddie was a guy from the U.S. that messaged me first. Usually I'm the one to reach out to people. But I clicked "like" on one of his posts and he PM'd me. Eddie was…unique. I've since stopped talking to him, but the stuff he told me was interesting, so I'm going to write it down.

Eddie claims he's a "collector of souls." He said it started happening when he turned 18. Whenever someone died in his small town, their soul would enter his body. He lives in some town in Texas. He said this scared him at first, but after a while, he got used to it. He says he would share part of that person's personality and some of their memories. He started doing better in school because he had a greater wealth of knowledge to draw from. And he'd suddenly possess new talents: painting, dancing, scuba-diving (yes, that was one of his examples).

The only thing was that every birthday he had, he'd lose all the souls, then start collecting them again from scratch. So after every birthday, he'd be dumb again until more people died and their souls joined him. He's now in his 40s and has gotten used to this. He said he's successful in his job, but he wouldn't tell me what he did for a living.

I have the feeling Eddie is full of shit. Something about the name "Eddie" makes a person seem untrustworthy. Maybe I'm just being prejudiced, but that was my first thought.

He was a strange man and started messaging me way too much, so I stopped responding. I think he got the hint because he doesn't message me anymore.

The knocking started again. All over the walls and roof. I yelled, "Stop!" and it stopped. It was quiet for half an hour, then started again.

I looked up paranormal investigators on the internet. I found one in Edmonton who seems cool, so I sent her an email telling her what's going on. Maybe she can help get rid of this. Her name is Addilyn. She lives in Sherwood Park. She had some videos on her website and she seems to know what she's talking about. She seems normal and calm.

I was still kind of nerve-wracking writing to her. I almost felt like I was doing something wrong. I even said, "I'm not making this up," which I realize now I shouldn't have said. But it seems like doubt is a huge part of this.

The knocking started again, louder than before. More of a pounding. All over the walls and roof. For some reason it never happens on the floor. The loud ones made me jump.

There was a knock at the front door and I went to look. It was my neighbour, asking me to stop pounding on the walls. I told him it wasn't me. I didn't have an explanation for it, so I just stood there like an idiot. Who else would it be? I live alone. I could tell he didn't believe me, but he was just like, "Ok," and went back to his apartment.

On top of everything else, my haunted life is affecting other people. Last thing I need is to get evicted and be homeless as well as broke and unemployed.

After that guy left, there was more knocking and I yelled, "Shut up!" It stopped. It seems to stop every time I yell at it (albeit temporarily), but it got me thinking that maybe it will do what I say. So I said, "Go away and never come back!" Now we wait and see if it works.

TUESDAY, NOVEMBER 12, 2019

It's been a couple days and there hasn't been any "activity." Maybe my assertiveness worked and whatever was here left. I feel better overall. I was able to sleep without much trouble the last couple nights. No sleeping pill or anything.

Dan finally texted me back. He's being weird. He said he's busy and can't talk. I don't know what he's busy with. He's in school, but he doesn't have a job. He doesn't do much except play video games and smoke weed. I'm not trying to put him down. He's a really great guy. He's always there for me and he's fun to hang around with. I'm just trying to put things in perspective.

But, yeah, that's what his text was: "Sorry, I'm really busy. I can't talk right now."

On another front, I have a job interview tomorrow at a clothing store at Southgate! If I get the job, I'm going to save my money and move to a different apartment. Hopefully the bad shit's stopped for good, but either way I want out of here.

I'm really nervous about the interview. I haven't done one in a while. I always worry I'll say stupid things. I guess the main thing is I can't look desperate.

Nothing scary better happen tonight that keeps me awake. I want to be rested and ready to go in the morning.

WEDNESDAY, NOVEMBER 13, 2019

It's time to go for the job interview. I'm practically trembling I'm so nervous. I'm worried they're going to ask why I'm not in school this year. I have to come up with a good excuse.

Remember, just walk in, stand up straight and present an air of confidence. Basically the exact opposite of how I really feel.

I ate a healthy breakfast, showered, did my makeup and dressed up, making sure I looked damn good. Sometimes I impress myself.

Wish me luck!

I'm back! It went so well! I was worried for nothing. The woman who interviewed me, Erin, was cool. I totally want to be like her when I grow up. When I got there, this other girl was just leaving her interview. Not to be mean, but just looking at her, I was like, "No way you're getting this over me." I could just tell by looking at her she wouldn't get the job. Don't tell me you don't think the same thing about people sometimes.

They did everything short of offering me the job. They asked when I could start and said they'd call me tomorrow. I'm so excited! I can finally get back to having a normal life and hopefully meet some new friends.

The apartment is freezing cold. It was fine a few hours ago when I wrote that last part after my interview, now it feels like I'm living in a frickin igloo.

First it was too hot in here, now it's too cold. I called the front office about it and left a message.

THURSDAY, NOVEMBER 14, 2019

Sometime during the night the temperature went back to normal. I went to bed with two extra blankets on the bed and woke up with the sheets soaked with sweat. I'll ask the front office if it's a heating problem. I hope it is and the ghost isn't controlling the temperature.

Something else happened that's strange. When I woke up, my phone was lying at the foot of the bed. I keep it on my nightstand next to the bed because that's where my charger is. So I don't see how it could get to the floor at the *bottom* of the bed. If I knocked it off in the middle of the night it would have fallen beside my bed, not at the foot of it. Of course there's still the rational explanation that I did it myself somehow.

I tried reaching out to Dan again but he still won't respond. I really miss him. Not just because I want someone to hang out with, but because he's such a good friend and I'm worried about him.

As I was typing that last sentence, my bedroom door opened on its own. No windows open or anything. Ugh. Why does this keep happening? My desk where I'm typing this is in the corner of the room and the door is behind me. Now I'm paranoid something's going to come in behind me when I'm not looking. I just got up and closed it.

It's weird. It seems like it's always the same things that move. My bedroom door opens and closes, but never the spare room or bathroom door (that I've seen). My closet has two sliding panels, one on each side. The left one will slide open or closed on its own sometimes, but never the right one. In the kitchen, it's always the cutlery drawer that opens on its own, and the two cupboards above it. But that's only

happened once or twice. There are four cabinets on each side of the kitchen but only

those two move. I wonder why that is.

I called the police officer who's working on the "Poe case." I asked if there was

any developments or suspects. He said there wasn't but he'd call me as soon as he had

something to report. I think he was hinting that I shouldn't contact him anymore.

They're probably not even working on it anymore. Too busy handing out traffic

tickets.

It's 9:00pm and that job never called. They said they'd call today. Maybe I'm

being too anxious, but I can't help it. I'm worried. Maybe somebody better than me

got interviewed after I left. (This is where you guys are supposed say, "That's

impossible, Genesis.")

I'm going to record myself sleeping, just to see if anything happens. Even though if

there is a ghost in my room while I'm sleeping, I'd almost rather not know about it,

but my curiosity has gotten the best of me.

FRIDAY, NOVEMBER 15, 2019

I recorded myself sleeping. It's weird watching yourself sleep. Nothing scary happened, but I toss and turn a lot in my sleep. I also sat up at one point and checked my phone. It looked like I was still half-asleep. I don't remember doing that.

That job emailed me and said they went with someone else. I don't know what happened. I was sure I had it. The email seemed very terse too. This is what it said:

Dear Genesis,

We went with someone else.

Erin

Uh…ok.

The other emails I got from her were super friendly; smiley-faces and exclamation points. "Looking forward to meeting with you!" "Thanks again for coming in, we'll be in touch tomorrow! :)" So I don't understand the sudden attitude shift. How much can change in two days? Maybe that's a form letter they send out to everyone who didn't get picked. I emailed them back and asked if there was a particular reason.

I guess I can't let it get to me. I'll keep sending out resumes. I didn't really want to work in a retail store anyways.

Check this out. Erin from that store wrote me back. This is her response to my inquiring about why I didn't get the job. I copied and pasted it from my email.

Genesis,

Honestly, we can't believe you have the audacity to ask us why you didn't get the job after what you did. Please do not contact us again.

Erin

Have they gone insane?! I emailed her back and asked what I did. Jesus, what the hell is going on? I didn't do *anything*. Everything was great after I left the interview. She even emailed me to thank me and say they'll be in touch. I've had no communication with them since.

I just heard a crash from the living room and went out there but nothing was out of place.

It must be a mistake. I can't think of a possible reason. I didn't lie on my resume, so it's not like they discovered something I wasn't truthful about. The only possibility I can think of is that Blythe had something to do with it. But there's no way she could have known I was looking for a job, let alone the exact place I interviewed at. Unless she followed me there. I did see her in my neighbourhood. It's possible. I still don't think that's the reason though.

I was in my room and I heard a glass smash in the kitchen. I went in and saw one of my glasses smashed on the floor. There's no way this wasn't the ghost. I did my dishes yesterday and they were all put away in the cupboards. So somehow the cupboard opened, the glass fell out, smashed on the ground and the cupboard closed again. Wish I could have gotten that on video.

And if anybody reading this thinks I'm making this up – fuck you for thinking that.

I decided to call my mom. I read these hauntings tend to happen with people under stress. Family problems cause stress. Maybe if I straighten out my family issues, it'll go away.

SATURDAY, NOVEMBER 16, 2019

I texted my mom and we're going to video chat in a couple hours. I'm not sure how it will go. It's always such a chore talking to her. I'm sure all moms are a nag to some degree, but my mom is positively evil. She's more like a fairy-tale stepmother than a real person. Everything she says is either a put-down, a back-handed compliment, or hiding some ulterior motive. It's emotionally exhausting spending time with her. Maybe she somehow subconsciously knew this and that's why she moved away. Like how bad mothers give their babies up for adoption if they can't care for them. Maybe my mom fucked right off to the other side of the country to spare me the pain of having to visit her every week.

Come to think of it, maybe this won't solve the haunting problem like I thought. My life is more likely to *improve* without contact with her. But she is my mom so I still have some obligation to keep her in my life.

I know this is terrible to say, but it is my journal so I have to be honest: I would much rather have had my mom die when I was a kid and have my dad still alive. He probably could have solved this whole problem on his own. I don't even know why he married my mom. I mean, I'm glad he did, otherwise I wouldn't be alive, but she treated him worse than she treated me. Supposedly he died of a heat attack, but I wonder if he just lost the will to live.

She would nag him constantly. One time he got laid off from his job and she was just relentless in her, "Get a job! You're so lazy! What kind of man can't support his family?!" bullshit. It wasn't his fault. She would bitch on and on about how we didn't have money, then she goes out shopping and buys $2000 worth of clothes right when dad wasn't working. I think she was trying to teach him a lesson that he better get a job soon. Bitch. He was only out of work for a month before he got a better job than he had before. My mom made it seem like it was the end of the world, all the while racking up debit, buying stuff for herself and telling us we couldn't have what we wanted for dinner because we were too poor.

Ugh. Maybe this video chat wasn't such a great idea. Oh, well. May as well get it over with.

I'm totally paranoid now. I keep thinking I see things out of the corner of my eye. Every noise is now suspect. Which sucks because I live in an apartment building with people all around. And next to a busy street. There's an apartment above, below and on each side of me. Every noise or voice makes my ears perk up (you know that feeling?) It's creepy. I hate it. Usually it's nothing, but sometimes it's not nothing. Sometimes it'll be an object I swear has been moved but can't quite remember. Other times it's more obvious. Doors and drawers opening and closing. It's like death by a thousand paper cuts. All these little things that creep me out are just driving me to the brink. Sometimes I think, "It's not that bad. It can't hurt me. I can live with it." Then it will happen and freak me out. It's always in the back of my mind. Just the anticipation that something's going to happen at any moment. At least I'm not hearing voices anymore. Or feeling that god-awful presence.

I just chatted with my mom. It went about as awesomely as I expected. I don't know why I never learn my lesson. It's always draining to talk to her, yet I do it again and again. I envy people who have normal parents.

The conversation basically went like this: the routine, "How are you doing?" "Good, how about you?" "Oh, you know, same old, same old." (This might be a good time to point out that I hate small talk and meaningless conversation. Maybe that's why I have such few friends – I prefer meaningful conversation and connection to boring, mindless chit chat. Any conversation that starts with, "So, what's new with you?" is going to be a chore to get through.)

Anyways, it took my mom all of fifteen seconds to get to, "Are you working?" This is the first time we've spoken in weeks and that's the first thing she asks me. Not, "How's your mental health?" "How's your feeling of wanting to throw yourself out your thirteenth floor window?" She was all, "I'm just curious. Don't get upset." I bet she *wanted* me to be unemployed just so she'd have a reason to nag me. One more thing to hold over me. I bet the only reason *she* has a job is she's sleeping with the boss. That might sound mean, but it did happen before. Maybe I'll tell that story later.

Then she was like, "Are you doing ok for money?" In her world if you have a job and a stable income, you're good to go. That's it. Doesn't matter how much of a catastrophe every other area of your life is in, as long as you have some job you hate and take home a paycheck there's no need to worry about you.

She said, "Well, if you don't have a job, what are you doing with your time? Since you're not in school?" Argh!!! Riiiiip! (That's the sound of me ripping my hair out by the roots.) My mother seriously can't think of something a person would do with their time other than work. How about: go to the gym, take an art class, dance, go for a run, go bungee jumping, go scuba diving, visit a friend, do volunteer work. There's a million things people can do! But her world is "work and save for retirement."

So, yeah, infuriating start to the conversation. However, it quickly took a turn for the bizarre. Mom said Dan called her! *My* Dan! My best friend, Dan! He called my mom! She said she didn't talk to him; she just saw that he called. She called him back but he didn't answer. What could Dan possibly want to talk to my mom for? I think he's only every met her twice. He's barely spoken to her. Maybe it was just a pocket dial, but how would he even have her number on his phone? This is really tripping me out. I texted him, asking why he called her, but I haven't heard back.

Towards the end of the conversation, something weird happened. My mom was talking and all of a sudden, her voice changed. It got deeper and a bit *growlier*. It freaked me out. I was like, "Mom, what's wrong with your voice?" She didn't know what I was talking about. Her voice went back to normal and that was pretty much the end of the conversation. So much for my plan of it making me feel better and less alone.

Just in case you feel I'm being too harsh, let me tell you about the time she dropped me off at school smelling like alcohol. I was in grade one and too young to really understand about alcohol. Mom drove me to school one morning and she walked me up to the door. My teacher, Mrs. Strahn, was there greeting the kids. My mom said something to her and Mrs. Strahn gave her this look of disgust. At the time I remember thinking it must be because my mom was ugly. For some reason I thought this was funny. Anyways, Mrs. Strahn asked to speak to my mom alone. She took her aside and my mom started yelling. "Mind your own fucking business!" and stuff like that. Finally, Mrs. Strahn came and took me inside. My mom just said, "I'll pick you up after school, Genesis."

I didn't want to ask my teacher what the fight was about because I'd learned to stay out of adult fights. After school, my dad was waiting to pick me up, which was unusual. I asked where mom was and he just grunted something. I could tell he was upset and we drove home in silence. I thought I was in trouble. Of course I wasn't.

As I got older, I finally got the full story. My teacher smelled alcohol on my mom's breath and confronted her about it, then called the cops. So mom got pulled over on her way home and was arrested for DUI. Yes, folks, my mom had more than the legal amount of alcohol in her system at eight in the morning. With her 7-year-old daughter in the car.

When I got home with dad, mom was there and she wasn't speaking. Nobody said anything the whole night. I knew something was up, but I didn't know what. My first thought was that mom and dad were getting divorced. Of course I thought that about everything at that age. Mom and Dad couldn't decide what restaurant to go to: they're getting divorced.

I don't know all the details, but mom had to go to court, but I think the charges got dropped or something. She managed to skirt any sort of punishment. But from then on, up until the time of his death, if Dad was home from work, *he* drove me. Otherwise, I walked. (The school wasn't very far.)

What kind of person puts a child in danger that way? I understand people have substance abuse problems, but you mess up your own life, you don't put other people in danger.

The stupid fire alarm went off again today. At least this time it wasn't my fault. But having to evacuate the building, wait for the fire department to come, then get everyone back up to their apartments is a pain in the ass. Not to mention, when the alarm goes off, it's blaring loud and always scares the shit out of me. I think it's happened four times since I've moved in here. A quarter of those times it was my fault. Lol.

One time the alarm went off and when I got to the lobby it was so smoky you could barely see two feet in front of your face. But it wasn't smoke, it was steam. A pipe had burst. I took a picture of it and posted it on social media. People were like, "Oh, my God, are you ok?!" It wasn't as bad as it looked.

The other times it happened, I think it was just stupid people (like me) burning something in the kitchen.

SUNDAY, NOVEMBER 17, 2019

I recorded myself sleeping last night and captured something disturbing. What looks like a hand quickly flashes past the bottom of the screen. I watched it frame by frame but it just looks like a blur. My first instinct is that it looks like someone waving their hand in front of the cam really quickly. It might be a technical thing, so I'm not totally freaking out, but it's something. I had my laptop on my desk, facing my bed. Tonight, I'm going to put it on my nightstand, facing the door.

I'm back on the sleeping pills to sleep. I'm almost out of those ones my mom left. I don't know if you can get them over-the-counter. If not, I'll see if I can get some from the doctor. If that's not possible, I might just have to beg my mom for more.

I finally heard back from the paranormal investigator. Addilyn is her name. She sent me a shitload of questions. Probably her way of weeding out the weirdos. There were obvious questions like: Are you on any medication? Have you ever been diagnosed with a mental illness? Have you ever been hospitalized for mental illness? Has a family member ever been hospitalized with a mental illness? To cut a long story short – *are you fucking crazy?* I didn't mention my mom's drinking, but other than that I don't think there's any history of that in my family tree.

There were other questions like, "Have you had a paranormal experience before? How often?" Then there was, "Have you ever seen a UFO? A bigfoot?" I assumed those questions were to filter out people who claim to see these things all the time. I told her I'd never seen any of those things or had anything even close to a paranormal experience until recently. I told her I don't really believe in it. Hopefully that scores me some brownie points.

There was one question I don't get: "Would you consider yourself interested or not interested in politics?" Uh…what? What does that have to do with being haunted? Are people interested in politics more likely to have paranormal experiences or less likely? I said I was "not interested," however I did vote in the last federal election.

Hopefully I'll hear back from her because I'm realizing this isn't going away on its own.

I finally heard back from Dan, but it's still really weird. This is the last text I sent him:

Dan, I'm really worried about you. I'd like to see you in person so we can talk things out. We've always been so close and now all of a sudden you seem distant and I don't know why. Did something happen? Did I offend you somehow? Are you angry with me? I just want to make sure you're ok. If you need someone to talk to you know I'm here for you. Let's get together for coffee. Please message me back. Hope you're doing well.

Finally, today, he responds with this:

Hi

That's it. *"Hi."* WTF? So I wrote back:

Hi, Dan. Did you read my message?

Now I begin the waiting process again. I hope I'm not coming across as needy. I'm not trying to control his life; I'm just worried about him as a friend. On the other hand, I have a lot to deal with in my own life, I can't be dealing with other people's problems too.

Ok, it's late and I'm going to bed. Nervous as fuck, but hopefully I'll sleep. I have my laptop on the nightstand, facing the door. Part of me doesn't want to get anything on video but part of me wants to. Goodnight.

MONDAY, NOVEMBER 18, 2019

Oh, my God, this is crazy! I watched the video from last night. At two hours and fourteen minutes a little boy crawls through the shot! Yes, I'm fucking serious! You could only see him for a split second when he passed my doorway, crawling down the hall towards the bathroom. But I paused it and it's definitely a little boy. He looks seven or eight and he's wearing a white shirt and black pants. Is he a ghost? Like, seriously…WTF?!!!! Is he the ghost of a kid who died in this apartment or something? My deadbolt is always locked so I don't see how a real kid could sneak in at three in the morning. He didn't look particularly scary. I'm not worried about him hurting me. It's just creepy.

I emailed the video the Addilyn, the paranormal lady. I told her it's escalating.

I needed to get out of the house for a bit, so I went out walking. Nothing else to do. Dan's not answering and Melinda's in B.C. for the week. I hate that I feel safer walking around the city than I do in my own home. There's a feeling in my apartment I don't like. Just walking in the door gives me the creeps. I don't know if it's just in my mind because of all the stuff that's been happening or if there's an actual negative energy in here. But seeing that little boy on camera is a definite indication that it's something physical. Or at least partly physical. I'm sleeping with my door closed from now on.

It also creeps me out because a lot of horror movies start with a little kid having an imaginary friend and shit gets bad quick. Then again, I'm not the age where kids have imaginary friends. And that shit wasn't imaginary. I got it on video!

I've seen a lot of the people who live in this building and I've never seen that kid before. Maybe I can ask Mrs. Pearson about it next time I see her.

I'm tempted to post the video online. "Real proof of ghost!" But people would probably accuse me of faking it. And what if it is some kid who lives in the building and snuck in here? His parents would be like, "What was our son doing in your apartment in the middle of the night?!" I don't want things turned around on me, so I'm keeping this quiet for now.

While I was out walking, I bought a bottle of wine. I plan to get drunk tonight. That should help take my mind off the chaos. And help me sleep.

I also set a trap. I poured bathtub cleaner, the white powder kind, in a thick line across the floor in the hall. So if Ghost Boy crawls through it, I'll know whether he has a physical presence of if he's more of a spectral being. Maybe he'll leave handprints.

I tried watching the Ghost Boy video again, but the file won't open. I just get an error message. That nagging doubt in the back of my mind again: did I *really* see a boy in the video?

It's 2am and I'm really drunk. I drank that whole bottle. I'm writing this part on my phone, lying on the couch. I'm waiting for Ghost Boy to come back so I can slap him. Can you go to jail for abusing a ghost kid? Lol.

TUESDAY, NOVEMBER 19, 2019

It's morning. I'm totally hungover. I got drunk by myself. I'm so cool. Life is awesome. Maybe I'm just following the example my mom set while I was growing up.

I left the camera running again but nothing happened. The powder is still there. I accidentally walked through it on the way to the bathroom, but there's no handprints or anything. Hopefully that was Ghost Boy's first and last appearance.

While we're on the subject of ghost children, this young kid from Texas (seems like a popular place for hauntings) sent me a video. It showed a security video image of a creepy-looking little girl in a dress, crawling on her hands and feet down a hallway. He said the girl is a ghost that's been following him around. The kid who sent the video is 12.

There's nothing about the video that leads me to believe the girl is a ghost. It's probably just his sister. The kid was like, "Do you believe me?" When someone says that, I immediately do not believe them. So I just said, "No." He never responded.

My Dad told me once that if someone is more concerned with you believing them than they are with whatever they're talking about, they're probably lying. He said over the years he learned the sure-fire way to tell someone's lying is if they say, "What? You don't believe me?" Makes sense to me. People who tell the truth will naturally assume you believe them, because, why wouldn't you? People who are always doubtful of others' trust are probably that way because people don't trust them. Usually because of a history of lying.

Point being – the Ghost Girl video was cool, but probably fake.

The water got shut off today. There was some sort of plumbing problem so they had to turn it off. I hate getting up in the morning and not being able to shower or brush my teeth. They finally turned it back on this afternoon.

THURSDAY, NOVEMBER 21, 2019

I spent the last couple days in a motel because I was too scared to sleep at home. Tuesday night that presence came back. It felt like it was following me around the apartment again. Wherever I went, it was right behind me. I could almost feel it breathing on my neck. It's hard to explain. I couldn't touch it but I could feel it there. I'd hear little breaths sometimes and a lip-smacking sound. You know that moist, smacking sound when you open and close your mouth? It was always like two inches from my ear. A couple times I said, "Go away!" and it backed off for a few minutes, then I'd feel it come right up behind me again. Once I said, "Please, God, make it go away," and it huffed. Very creepy.

Then my bedroom door and the cutlery drawer in the kitchen started opening and closing on their own. It happened a bunch of times, like maybe seven or eight. There was pounding and thudding on all the walls. But that sinister presence was the worst. Even though I couldn't see it, I somehow knew it was standing there, smiling at me. Not a friendly smile, like the most evil smile ever. It's like I could see it without seeing it. If that makes any sense.

I finally couldn't take it anymore. No way I could sleep with that thing there, especially when it would follow me into my room. So I left. I drove to the Westmount area and found a cheap motel. The guy gave me a deal - $90/night. I'm not sure why he gave me the deal, but I'm not gonna ask questions when getting a sweet discount.

I was in a super bad mood when I got there. There were these two guys smoking outside. One said, "How's it going, sweetheart?" I just said, "Fuck off." They laughed. Fucking assholes. But I felt good for saying something. Usually I don't.

It felt good to be away from the apartment. Like a vacation from my horror life. I pretty much just spent two days watching TV. I went to West Edmonton Mall for a bit yesterday. And I ate way too much McDonalds (there was one across the street from the motel.) But it was like a mini poor-person vacation. I would have stayed longer, but I'm low on money.

There was a huge spider in my room that I killed. I hate spiders. I haven't had any in my apartment since I moved in. I think it's because I'm high up and spiders have no reason to go up there. I've had cockroaches and a couple ladybugs (which I thought was weird).

This couple in the room next to me started fighting. At one point some guy from another room came out and yelled for them to shut up. The couple fighting was like, "Fuck you!" And the other guy was like, "Come out here and say that!" Then they were arguing back and forth. Someone must have called the cops because they showed up. I don't know if anybody got arrested. I couldn't see out my window. But it was quiet after that. I guess that's the kind of people you get in cheap motels in this area.

When I went to McDonalds the first night, I passed one of those guys who was harassing me earlier in the parking lot. He apologized for his friend, who was apparently drunk. He said he wouldn't do it again. For some reason that made me feel better.

There's a bar in the same parking lot as the motel. I stopped by, thinking I'd maybe have one drink. And I just wanted to be around people, but not necessarily talk with them. I went in and I could tell it was a bunch of regulars. They were all over 40 and looked at me like, "What the hell is this young girl doing in here?" I turned around and left. Lol.

Luckily there's a liquor store in the same parking lot too, so I bought some coolers and drank them while watching movies.

It might seem like I'm drinking too much, but I swear, it's only because of the constant fear. I don't like getting drunk that much. If my apartment wasn't haunted, I definitely would not be drinking this much. Being drunk = no fear (or *less* fear). It's as simple as that.

I wonder if the guy at the motel front desk thought I was a criminal on the run. Or a drug addict? Or a prostitute? What kind of young woman randomly sleeps in a cheap motel for no reason? I definitely didn't fit in with the other clientele there. I guess they're used to not asking questions.

Now that I'm home, I feel a little better. The apartment doesn't seem as scary now. I've been analyzing what happened. The Ghost Boy isn't tall enough to breathe on the back of my neck. I'm six feet tall. And yes, I know that's tall, I don't need to hear it for the millionth time. So that must mean there's more than one ghost in here. Maybe it's a man and his son. Maybe they're people that died here at some point? How do you find out about the previous tenants in an apartment? Just *knowing* might be the first step to getting rid of them.

I've been reading about hauntings and other people's experiences. The consensus is that the phenomena can't physically hurt you, even if it is scary. So maybe I can learn to live with it. The only thing I absolutely cannot live with is that presence. Everything else pales in comparison. Maybe if I ignore it, it will go away?

Dan's parents messaged me yesterday to see what's going on with him. He hasn't been talking to them either. I told them he's ignoring me too. I wonder if he's gotten himself addicted to drugs or something like that. I really can't think of any reason he'd just vanish like this. I wish he could just send me a simple text telling me what's going on. I texted him a couple times from the motel and he hasn't responded.

I thought maybe he was acting like this because something paranormal happened to him when he was at my place that last time. But that can't be because he was happy and normal when he left to go to that birthday party. This didn't start until after that. Maybe something happened to him at that party? But still, why wouldn't he tell me about it?

Addilyn, the paranormal lady, finally emailed me back and said she could come meet me, but she's not free until next Thursday. So I guess I just have to fend for myself until then. She never said anything about the video, so I don't know if she watched it or not. All her emails are very short and to the point. I just want to pour my heart out to her and tell her everything that's been going on and all my thoughts and feelings on it. I just want her to tell me it's not a big deal and it will go away soon.

I just got back from the grocery store and ran into Mrs. Pearson outside. She lives on my floor, down the hall from me. I don't know her first name. She's lived here for a long time. I asked her about previous tenants who lived in my apartment. I asked if there had ever been any kids living here or a father and son. She said a mother and her 7-year-old son lived in my apartment for a few months several years ago. I asked if the boy died and she gave me a weird look and said no. So that doesn't really solve anything. It's probably not even them.

I'm tempted to go to the rental office and ask about all the people who lived here before me, I just can't think of a good reason to justify why I'm asking. And there's probably privacy laws against it.

The other day when the fire alarm went off, I talked to some guy outside who lives in the building. I was trying to find out if there was weird shit going on in his apartment. My thinking was that maybe this is going on everywhere in the building and it's not just me. I mean, why would a ghost be confined by the physical walls of one apartment? I couldn't come up with a non-weird way of bringing it up, so I asked him if he'd been hearing knocks and pounding in his apartment. He said no. I brushed it off and said, "Must just be construction in the apartment above me."

It happened again. Another glass fell off the kitchen counter when I was in my room and shattered on the floor. When I went out to see it, the cutlery drawer slid open on its own. I closed it and took out my phone to see if I could record it happening again, but it didn't. I don't know why this thing likes the dishes so much. I just wish it would stop breaking shit I have to pay to replace. I sent the video of the glass to Addilyn. I'm hoping she sees it's an emergency and can make time sooner than next week.

Maybe I should invite a bunch of people over for a party so they can see this weird shit. Then they'd believe me and I wouldn't feel so isolated. God, I'm pathetic.

I was sitting in the living room and I heard the cutlery drawer open again in the kitchen. I turned around and all the cupboards and drawers were open! I went and closed them but when I closed the cupboard above the sink (where I keep the glasses), there was resistance, like someone was pushing on it from the other side.

I've seen this exact cupboard thing happen in movies before. I've been reading that poltergeist activity is caused by the person themselves. Like subconsciously. So did this just happen because I saw it in movies? Am I the cause of this whole thing? Or rather, my subconscious? It better not be *me* or I'll be super pissed at myself.

As a test, I tried focusing really hard on making the kitchen drawer open, to see if I could move it with my mind, but it didn't work. Of course. That would be cool, though, to have telekinetic powers.

It's four in the morning. I can't sleep. I'm really scared. At least I don't feel the physical presence like I did before. I'm just scared something will happen. I'm watching this really weird Italian movie with subtitles. I can't follow what the hell is going on, but it's somehow still intriguing to me. You ever been so tired you can't sleep? That's me now.

Weird. I looked up this Italian movie on the internet and the director committed suicide this past Monday. I wonder if that's why they're playing his movie. Or maybe it's just a coincidence.

FRIDAY, NOVEMBER 22, 2019

I finally fell asleep on the couch and slept until noon. Every time I manage to sleep seems like a small victory. Like a, "Fuck you. You can't keep me from sleeping," to the ghost. Things are less scary in the light of morning. A new day is a new opportunity. At least I'm waking up. Some people go to sleep and never wake up. It's depressing that I take solace in *not dying* in my sleep but when your life is shit, you take what you can get. At least I'm trying to put a positive spin on things. I keep telling myself, "All this will be over one day. I just have to hang in there."

Still no word from Dan. So I decided I'm going to be a good friend and go to his place tomorrow to check on him.

I needed to get out of the house. So Melinda and I are going out for drinks. It's Friday night after all. I haven't been to a club in months. I only have $18 in my bank account but I just need to get out. Maybe it'll be fun. Better than spending another night in the house, slowly becoming a hermit.

I'm home from the bar. I'm pretty drunk. I didn't spend any money because these guys bought us drinks all night. I had a good time. Took my mind off things. I think Melinda went home with one of the guys we were with. She was all over him the whole night. I thought he was gross but I guess people have their own tastes.

One guy was trying to hit on me but I made it clear I wasn't interested. I spent most of the time talking with this guy named Cal. I'm pretty sure he was gay but it might have just been because he didn't come on to me. He started some tech company. I can't remember what it was, I didn't really understand, but maybe he'll be the next Bill Gates and I'll be like, "Hey! I know that guy!"

As we were leaving, the guy I wasn't interested in asked what I was doing. I said, "It's two in the morning. I'm going home." He was like, "Ok, cool," and stood there like he was waiting for me to invite him. I just turned around and left. Melinda laughed.

Just a few minutes ago I was in the living room eating pizza and these papers I had on the table blew off. But the window was open, so I'll assume that's what it was.

First thing tomorrow, I'm going to clean and organize my apartment. I've been neglecting that since all this started. But if I'm in a situation I can't control, the least I can do is keep my personal life organized. A clean house is on top of that list. Cleanliness is godliness, as the saying goes.

SATURDAY, NOVEMBER 23, 2019

This is weird. I was cleaning my storage closet and I found this thing behind my bike. It's a little triangle made of twigs, held together with tape. And there's some red hair attached to it. It looks like my hair. And it looks like it's burned. What the fuck is this thing and how'd it get in my storage room? Nobody's been in my apartment. That I know of. Dan was here before he started acting weird, but he never went in the storage room. The maintenance guy came by to fix the heating when I wasn't home, but why would he leave this? Maybe I should go tell the front office. Just in case.

I just went downstairs to the rental office. The maintenance guy was there and he said he didn't leave it here. I believe him. Is this some sort of witchcraft shit that someone...someone being *Blythe*...put here to put a curse on me? I read about stuff like that. She was pissed off at me and she's into all that weird shit. And it makes sense with what she was saying about me not sleeping and being sorry she can't stop it. I'm tempted to message her and ask, but she hasn't contacted me in a couple weeks and I want to keep it that way.

If it was her, how'd she get in my apartment? And how'd she get my hair? If it even is my hair. This really creeps me out. I'm getting bad vibes from it. I'm going to get rid of it.

I just got back from the River Valley where I threw that thing into the river. If it was the cause of this haunting, maybe it will stop now that it's gone.

On my way there (it's a ten-minute walk from my house) I passed a man with a dog and the dog started viciously barking at me, just like that other time. The guy yelled at his dog (Benji) to calm down. I'm starting to be afraid of dogs now. Maybe the twig thing gave off vibes imperceptible to humans. After I chucked it in the river, on the way back, I passed the same guy as he was leaving the park and the dog barely noticed me. The guy apologized again.

Hopefully this is the end of this little adventure *(nightmare)*.

I totally forgot to check on Dan today. Some friend I am.

I got a message from Michelle. She was the one with the roommate, Dani, who started calling herself "Big Man Carl." She said there was an incident and the police shot Dani! She died. Michelle hadn't heard from Dani since she moved out. She heard about what happened in the news. I looked it up online, just to see if it was true. Looks like it is. The reports didn't say her name, but they said a woman was shot by police after she was attacking people on the street with a sword (!) That's crazy. I hope that's not in my future – getting possessed and shot by police.

More craziness. Everything was calm tonight and I was feeling pretty good. I was reading, which I haven't done in a while because I haven't been able to concentrate. Then all of a sudden, I heard a baby crying. It was faint but definitely a baby. It sounded like it was coming from inside the apartment, but wherever I went to look for it, it always sounded like it was coming from far away. If I went to the bathroom, it was coming from the living room. If I went to the living room, it sounded like it was coming from the bedroom. When I went to the bedroom, it was coming from the bathroom. Not 100% sure it was paranormal. Maybe it was coming from another apartment. But I haven't heard any babies around here before. It didn't freak me out that much. Compared to other stuff that's happened, it's not that bad.

Nothing weird happened last night after the baby crying. But I ran into Mrs. Pearson in the elevator and she said there's a family with a baby that moved in above me. So that explains the baby crying. Although it really sounded like it was coming from inside the apartment.

Anyways, I'm going to go check on Dan. I'll be back soon.

I just came back from Dan's place. His car was gone, but his front door was unlocked, which is not like Dan at all. I went in and called his name. I looked all around but he wasn't there. All his stuff was there, including his phone. He never leaves home without his phone. Who does? He doesn't have roommates so there's nobody to ask. I saw a neighbour outside when I left. I asked him if he'd seen Dan recently but the guy just stared at me with a blank stare. I don't think he spoke English.

I texted Dan's mom and they haven't heard from him since they messaged me the other day. I feel bad for his parents. They're the nicest people ever. So I don't know where Dan is. I'm wondering if I should call his school and ask if he's been showing up. Should I file a missing person's report? I don't want to look like I'm overreacting. Maybe he's fine. Maybe he just went to the store and I broke into his house. He's a grown man. He doesn't have to talk to me if he doesn't want to. But some sort of explanation would be nice. I just have this really bad feeling about it. I can't explain it, I just have this feeling that it has something to do with my haunting. Just like the job thing. It's not normal. In the pit of my stomach I know it's all connected. I just don't know how.

Of course, I could be totally wrong.

Wow. Shit's really happening now! I happened to glance out my window and there's this little patch of grass next to the visitor parking lot. There was a little girl running around on it, on her hands and feet. Just like in the video that kid from Texas sent me! Is it the same girl? They both had long, blonde hair and were wearing a dress. Although, in the video, she was wearing a grey dress and this girl was wearing a blue one.

I went downstairs and walked out into the parking lot to see her up close, but she was gone. So I don't know if that's the same girl or if it's just a coincidence. If it's the same girl, it has to be paranormal. But what's the link to Texas? Is it just because I watched that video?

It's like there's a whole family. That scary presence seems like a man, even though I haven't actually seen him/it yet. Then there's a little boy, a little girl and maybe a baby. I don't mind if they're outside. I just don't want them coming into my apartment.

The little girl doesn't seem threatening, she just looks creepy because of the way she moves - on her hands and feet with her butt up the air. It's unnerving. I hope I don't see her again.

I dropped my phone on the street today and cracked the screen! Son of a bitch! I don't even have enough money to fix it. I need a job. Soon.

MONDAY, NOVEMBER 25, 2019

The police just left. It was the same cop as last time, but he was with a partner. The partner was older and I immediately didn't like him. He was giving me this cold look like I was under interrogation or something. Good cop, bad cop routine? They said they were following up on the Poe case, but they asked me if I knew a guy named Dale Bardem. Apparently, he was murdered. I've never heard of him and I told them that.

I never pay attention to the news. I stopped a few years ago. It's too depressing and I hate the media. But I just wanted to see if there was anything about this Dale Bardem guy. Apparently, he was stabbed to death in an alley on 118th Ave. There wasn't much information other than that.

I asked the cops if they suspect he's the one that killed my dog. They said they didn't know. It's just something they were looking into. So I don't know what's going on, but it's disconcerting that I'm being asked about a murder victim.

As they were leaving, the older cop was like, "We'll be in touch if we have any more questions." Uh…*what other questions*? I just want to know who killed my fucking dog, not about some gang member that was killed on the North Side. (I don't really know that he was a gang member. I'm just speculating.)

It continues. I came out of the bathroom tonight and got this chill up my spine. I just had this feeling that something was outside my apartment door. I looked through the peephole and there was this weird-looking guy standing at the end of my hall, staring at my door. I took a picture through the peephole with my phone. The picture looks creepier than seeing him for real for some reason. Too bad you can't make out his face in it. He was standing there in that spot for at least ten minutes!

After he left, I went out to look (I couldn't help myself). I peeked around where the elevators are and he suddenly stepped out from around the corner! I burst out, "Oh shit!" and fucking ran back into my apartment and locked the deadbolt. I looked through the peephole and the guy came right up to my door and stood there. I ran into my room and called building security. By the time they showed up, the guy was gone, but I showed them the picture and they filled out a report. They said they'd keep an eye out and that I should call them if he comes back.

Is he another ghost? Or some creep stalking me? I didn't recognize him. Now I'm scared to leave the apartment. Wonderful. I'm scared to be *in* the apartment and to leave. One way to look at it is that the ghost(s) in my apartment can't hurt me. A real-life man can. So maybe I'm safer inside.

I wish Dan was here.

TUESDAY, NOVEMBER 26, 2019

Nothing else happened last night. I eventually fell asleep on the couch, watching TV. I bought some sleeping pills at the drugstore, but I need stronger stuff.

I woke up to this text from Melinda:

Hey, Gen, do you by any chance have my I.D.? It's missing from my wallet and I remember you were looking in my wallet when we went to the bar. Just wondering if you took it by mistake.

Uh, no, Melinda, I didn't take your fucking I.D. I went in your wallet because you asked me to grab you cash because you were too busy making out with that guy at the table. So, no, I don't have it. That pissed me off. But I guess I should be nice. Can't lose any more friends. I wrote back and said I didn't have it.

Maybe I'm reading too much into things, but this isn't the first time recently that I've been accused of something.

I'm flush with cash again. I sold a bunch of my stuff at a pawn shop. Jewelry, my old guitar and stuff. Made $400. Not bad. I also bought a cross to put around my neck from a Christian store. I'm not religious, but my views on life and the universe have changed drastically with everything that's been happening. I'm not expecting it to help much, but it's worth a shot. I considered getting a crucifix with the Jesus on it, but they creep me out. So I'll try this. If it doesn't work, maybe I'll upgrade.

I finally got a text from Dan! He just said, "It won't work." That's it. Which makes no sense with the last text I sent him. My first thought was that he was talking about the cross. Which would be really freaky. How could he possibly know? But he sent the text *before* I bought it. I sent him back a bunch of question marks. Of course, he hasn't responded. I'm thinking of going to his house again and waiting for him.

No sign of the guy in the hall but every time I leave the apartment, I'm scared he's going to step out of the elevator or something.

More craziness! I had a shower tonight and after I got out, I heard a little girl giggling out in the hall. I opened the bathroom door and, of course, there was nobody there. I heard the giggling coming from all around but I could never find the source. Just like with the crying baby. I was walking around, trying to find it and all of a sudden, my bedroom door slammed shut. I've almost gotten used to the opening and closing doors but this was a full-on *slam*. With force. I don't like it. I went in and looked around my room (under the bed first) and there was nothing there.

Maybe it's the girl from outside (and Texas) that was giggling, but that girl looks to be about 10. The giggling sounded like a 3-year-old. But it doesn't mean they're not related. I have no idea. Either way it was fucking creepy.

WEDNESDAY, NOVEMBER 27, 2019

I feel so much better today. In spite of everything, I had such a good sleep and feel so rested. Thank you sleeping pill and two glasses of wine. You now how when you're rested and refreshed, you feel like you can take on the world? That's how I feel. Like maybe things won't be so bad after all. Maybe that's what this whole haunting is about. If it is an intelligent entity doing it, maybe they try to scare you so you can't sleep. If fucks with your mind and you start to lose hope. I guess I have to do everything in my power to make sure that doesn't happen.

Maybe this will be a positive experience when all is said and done. Maybe years from now I'll look back and laugh. Maybe in the future there won't be such a stigma around this stuff and I'll feel confident telling the story. Maybe my grandkids will be amused by it. When they're older. I don't want to scare the shit out of them.

Maybe my story will be made into a movie! Who would play me? Maybe Charlize Theron! I know she's quite a bit older than me, but I love her! Maybe I'm getting too ahead of myself.

Ok, you'll never believe what happened. Pretty much right after I finished writing that last segment, there was a knock at my door. It was Melinda. She dropped by unannounced, which is strange. I had the feeling something was up right away. She said she was in the area and stopped by to see what I was up to. We were just sitting around, talking, but she was being weird. It was like she was mad at me and was pretending to be nice. I just got a cold vibe from her. I was hoping she'd leave, but I didn't want to kick her out. We had this awkward, boring conversation for twenty minutes or so, then I went to the bathroom. When I came back, she was standing in the living room, holding her I.D. Yes, the I.D. she supposedly lost and accused me of taking. She flipped out, saying she found it under my couch. There's no way it was under the couch. I'm the only one who's been in here and I live alone. And I sure as hell didn't put it there. I've cleaned the floors since we went to the bar and I would have noticed it. It was 100% not under my couch. So she was screaming at me, calling me a thief. The people in the next apartment starting pounding on the wall for us to shut up. I finally just told her to get out and she left.

She obviously put it there herself. But why would she do that? It doesn't make sense. We're supposed to be friends. Why would she falsely accuse me of stealing something? Then drive all the way here, wait until I leave the room and pretend she found it under the couch. It just doesn't make sense. But the fact is, I know *I* didn't put it there and it was really "convenient" that she just happened to show up out of the blue for no reason and wait until I was in the bathroom to "find" her missing thing. It's baffling. But I think it's safe to say we're not friends anymore.

I really, really, really, miss Dan. And to tell you the truth, I miss Blythe too. I miss the good Blythe, not the psycho, witch Blythe.

I was just reading about something called apportation. It's the teleportation of objects from one location to another. Apparently, it's been reported in paranormal cases. People have had objects move from one room to another, even from one house to another. I read one story where this family kept having objects appear in their house that belonged to their next-door-neighbour. Maybe this is what happened with Melinda's I.D. and the hair triangle twig thing. I have no other explanation for how they magically appeared in my apartment. (Other than the completely logical explanation that someone put them there). It seems unlikely that objects teleported across the city, into my home, but you never know. However, if this is going to be happening, it would be cool if it was money or other useful stuff!

This is insane! I started hearing the knocking again and I tried knocking back, like trying to communicate with it and it seems to be working. I started knocking in a certain pattern, and it would imitate me. That proves it's a sentient entity, doesn't it? (Unless I'm an idiot and it's someone in the next apartment doing it. But I don't think so.) The knocking sounded like it was coming from the spare bedroom and I was knocking back on the wall next to my computer desk, which shares a wall with the spare bedroom.

Anyways, after playing the knocking game for a bit, I said out loud, "I'm going to ask questions. Answer with one knock for yes, two for no." The following is my best attempt at transcribing the conversation.

Is my name Genesis? (One knock)

Is my name...Darlene? (Two knocks.) I asked this to make sure the first answer wasn't just a fluke. This "false" question confirms it can think.

Do I live in London? (Two knocks)

Do I live in Australia? (Two knocks)

Do I live in Edmonton? (One knock)

Are you a ghost? (Two knocks)

Are you a demon? (Two knocks) Although there was a painfully long wait
before these knocks. On the other hand, several questions had a long wait
before a reply. Not sure it means anything.

Are you alive? (Two knocks)

Are you dead? (Two knocks)

So what are you? No reply. (Probably because it can only answer yes or no.)

Did you choose to haunt my apartment on purpose? (Two knocks)

Did you choose to haunt ME on purpose? (One knock)

What do you want with me? (Forgot it had to be yes or no)

Do you have good intentions towards me? (Two knocks) Not good.

You have bad intentions towards me? (One knock) Uh oh.

Do you intend to hurt me? (One loud thump) Fuck.

Do you want to kill me? There was a long time with no reply.

Are you refusing to answer that question? (One knock)

Will you ever leave? (Two knocks)

Is there anything I can do to make you leave? (One knock)

Can you please stop bothering me? (Two knocks) But these knocks didn't come from the spare room like the others, they came from the hallway outside my room.

So that was the craziest thing ever. I was actually talking to a non-human entity! The conversation ended abruptly after it knocked from the hall. I asked it more stuff after that, but it didn't answer. Guess it was busy. It was strange that I asked it if it would ever leave and it said no, but then I asked it if I could *do* something to make it leave and it said yes. I might have to be crafty with it because it might be deceitful. I take these answers to mean that if it has its way, it won't leave, but there *is* a way to force it out. This isn't random shit happening, this is a thing than can think. I don't know what it is. It says it's not a ghost or a demon.

But can we agree that it's official – the whole thing isn't just in my head?

The good thing is Addilyn, the paranormal woman, is coming tomorrow. Hopefully she can give me advice and tell me how to get rid of it.

I'm thinking of going to the liquor store to pick up something to help me pass out. I'm not sure the sleeping pills are going to be enough on their own.

Right as I was sitting in my living room, typing that last part, a kitchen cupboard opened on its own. I went and closed it and as soon as I sat down, the bathroom light flicked on on its own. I went to turn the light off and said out loud, "Can you cut this out? I'm sick of getting up every two seconds?"

THURSDAY, NOVEMBER 28, 2019

I eventually slept last night, but not much. Addilyn is supposed to be here in an hour. I tried to confirm the time with her this morning and she never responded, but hopefully she's still coming. I'm a stickler for keeping appointments. I confirm everything. Even if it's just me and Dan meeting somewhere to hang out, I always text him to say, "Hey! We still meeting at (wherever) at 2?" If people don't confirm plans closer to the date, I assume they'll forget. Which they frequently do. Yes, I'm neurotic. I can live with that.

After Addilyn leaves, I'm going to go to Dan's house again. I feel selfish for just worrying about myself and ignoring him. Obviously, he's got something going on.

Addilyn just left. That was a big waste of time. At least it didn't cost anything. She's way different than in her videos. As soon as I let her in, she started looking around my apartment and I could just feel her judging everything. Like, sorry, I don't live in a huge, nice house with maid. I'm a broke ex art student.

When she looked in my storage closet, she made this "tisk" sound like she was disappointed. I don't know what she was talking about. It's not that messy in there. I wanted to punch her.

We sat down in the living room and started talking. I tried telling her about all the stuff that happened but she didn't seem interested. She kept cutting me off. Part of the reason I invited her over was to pour all this out onto someone. Get it off my chest. I haven't been able to tell anyone. Writing this journal helps a bit, but I wanted to tell an actual human being. I figured since she's in this line of work, she'd be understanding. I get it, she probably hears this shit all the time, but she could have at least humoured me.

So she ended up giving me this little speech that just sounded like some standard lecture she gives to everyone. It definitely wasn't tailored to my specific case. She said the entity is likely what's called a "parasite" in her field. Religious people call it a demon. (It said it *wasn't* a demon though). She told me to stop communicating with it. No knocking, no talking, definitely no seances or anything like that. She says sometimes it goes away on its own or the "disturbances" start happening so infrequently you just stop noticing. But other times she said a parasite can attach itself to a person for years or even to a family for generations.

I told her about the twig/hair thing and asked if that could be the cause. She said it's possible. If someone used that thing as a conduit to put a curse on me, it could have "opened a portal" that let this entity in. A year ago I would have laughed and not believed a second of this. Now, I'm not so sure.

She also said that moving wouldn't help because it would just follow me. She said most cases she works on involve *people* that are haunted, not places. I didn't even know that was possible. She said sometimes inanimate objects, usually furniture or pieces of art or sculptures, can be haunted. She also said it's rare, but sometimes animals can be haunted. I told her about Poe but she just dismissed it like it didn't interest her. Bitch.

While she was talking, there was a knock on the wall coming from my room. She said, "Is there anyone else here?" Uh…you just looked in my room ten minutes ago and there was nobody there. I told her I was alone. Then the best thing in the world happened – my cutlery drawer opened on its own. She turned to look at it, then looked back at me. The look on her face was anger at first, like somehow I had done something. But the look turned to horror as the reality of what just happened dawned on her. She immediately started wrapping things up. I asked what I could do to get rid of it. She asked if I was religious. I'm not. I showed her the cross, but said I just bought it on a whim, "just in case." She said sometimes a "cleansing" or "home exorcism" can work if a person is religious. If they're not, it can make it worse. So basically, she told me to be positive, happy and live *normally* (whatever that means).

She left. I watched her walk to the visitor parking lot through my window and she sat in her car for half an hour before leaving. I don't know what she was doing.

So in conclusion, I waited all that time and got my hopes up for nothing. Her advice is "be positive and hope it goes away." Wonderful.

I went to Dan's again. I don't even know if he's been back since I last went there. His car wasn't there again and the door was still unlocked. His house looked exactly the same. The same chip bags and stuff on his coffee table. I looked around for him again and I swear I heard footsteps walking around but I looked everywhere and there was no sign of him. I tried looking (aka snooping) on his phone, but I don't know his password. I can't file a missing person's report, can I? I don't think you can use the police to track down your friend who isn't talking to you. And I'd rather limit my meetings with the police anyways.

My cross suddenly started feeling really hot. It wasn't too bad at first, but then it got hotter and hotter to the point I couldn't touch it. So I took it off and set it my desk. As an experiment, I poured a cold glass of water and lowered the cross into it. (The chain wasn't hot, just the cross). The water sizzled and bubbled and it made this "tsssssss" sound. It was crazy. After that, the cross wasn't hot anymore so I put it back on. An hour later I went back into the kitchen. I'd left the glass on the counter and the water had turned black! Like *jet black*. I dipped my finger in it and it was thick, like syrup. It didn't smell like anything but it took the whole night before the black stuff was completely washed off my finger. Very strange. Maybe that means the cross is working? I'm not sure. It must be having some effect.

A couple new updates. First up - I tried calling my mom because I was lonely. And a man answered. That in itself isn't that big of a deal. Maybe she has a new boyfriend. She's had an endless string of losers in her life since Dad died. What makes it scary is that it sounded exactly *like* my dad. Who died when I was twelve. So…yeah. I don't know what to think about that. He answered and I asked for my mom. He said she's not in right now and asked who was speaking. I didn't want to tell him, so I just said I'd call back and hung up. I'll never get my dad's voice out of my head and that *was* his voice. Hopefully my mom calls back soon and tells me it's some other guy. That will make me feel so much better.

SATURDAY, NOVEMBER 30, 2019

It's been quiet since Thursday. Nothing paranormal happened except a few knocks that I ignored. Maybe it's starting to go away. Of course I've thought that before.

No call from my mom. I texted her again asking if she's free to talk. I bet she just loves that I'm practically begging to talk to her.

Nothing from Dan either, but that doesn't seem so unusual anymore.

However, the good news: I got another job interview! It's for a receptionist position at a tech company (I don't want to name them because what if someone publishes my journal and they sue me. Lol). They do coding and stuff. Basically, things I don't understand, but don't need to. I'll just be answering phones and filing and stuff. It's pretty close to here on Calgary Trail. I'm not getting my hopes up, but it pays better than that last job so...hope, hope.

The plot thickens. My mom finally called me back and get this – Dan went to see her! In Thunder Bay, Ontario! It's like a three-day drive! She said he just showed up at her house, upset and crying. I asked her what was wrong with him but she wouldn't tell me. She said Dan asked her not to tell anyone and she won't betray his trust. Yeah, great, Mom. Since when are you a fucking saint? The one time you're trying to be honest and protect someone's feelings is when you know it's torturing me.

What was the point of her even telling me? Just because she knew it would bother me? I was like, "Mom, he's my best friend. You have to tell me what's wrong with him." She was like, "You can't be *that* good a friend if he doesn't trust you enough to confide in you." Urgh! I wanted to strangle her!

After I realized it was a hopeless cause, I just told her to tell Dan I love him and miss him and really want to talk. She just said, "Fine."

So I don't know if Dan's coming back to Edmonton now or if he's staying in Thunder Bay. Maybe I should just forget about him. If he wants to reach out to me or come back into my life, he can. If not, there's not much I can do about it.

I asked her about a man answering her phone and she just said, "There's no man here, Genesis." So I'm assuming it was a paranormal incident. Which raises the question, how does this "parasite" or whatever it is, know what my dad sounds like? Can it read my thoughts? That's kind of disturbing to think about.

It feels like there's a conspiracy against me. Everyone's doing shit behind my back. Why would Dan drive across the entire country to go to my mom and not me? What the hell is he upset about? Melinda accuses me of stealing, that other job accuses me of doing *something*. The police are questioning me about a murder! You can't tell me there's not something strange going on. My first instinct is that it's all connected to this haunting. But how? It doesn't seem like it can be.

I texted Dan and told him to contact me. I was a little firmer than I've been previously. Not quite an ultimatum but getting close.

More drama. I got a text from Melinda, asking if I was outside her house last night. Which I wasn't. I told her that. I'm almost starting to detest all this melodrama worse than the haunting.

Almost.

I had an idea about that freaky dude in the hall. The cops asked me about that guy who was murdered, Dale Bardem. I thought maybe that dude was his ghost or something. So I Googled his name and...*dun, dun, dun*...it's not him. They look nothing alike. So back to square one.

Anyways, I'm going to relax all day tomorrow and probably won't update my journal. I'll update you Monday if anything happens. I also have my job interview Monday. Wish me luck!

MONDAY, DECEMBER 2, 2019

That was a hard interview! Probably the hardest I've ever had. They asked me all these scenario questions like, "What would you do if you were dealing with a customer who became abusive?" Stuff like that. Makes me wonder what kind of job it is. Some of the questions were hard: "Describe a situation where you used teamwork to overcome a problem." I made up bullshit stories for most of them. I don't have much work experience so I don't have a lot to draw from. And I'm not really a "team" kind of person. I prefer to work alone. But I'll work with whoever I damn-well have to to get a paycheque. I think every job interview involves some level of deceit. Kind of like a first date. You put on this persona to cast yourself in the best possible light. And it takes a few weeks of working (or a few dates) before the "real" person comes out.

I think it went ok, though. The guy who interviewed me was kind of weird-looking. He reminded me of a bulldog. His name was "Doug." I don't know why, but I hate that name. Doug. It just sounds like "dug." So redneck and dumb. Doug. *Doug.* Ok, I'm being ridiculous. I'm sure he's a lovely man. I hated his tie, though. I couldn't stop staring at it. I had to constantly remind myself, "Look him in the eye. Don't look at his tie."

Hopefully I'll get this job. They said they had other people to interview and they'd be in touch. So I guess I just wait. And hopefully no mysterious force interferes on my behalf.

I've been stretching my dollars so much lately that getting a paycheque will be a fortune. It'll seem like I'm rich all of a sudden. Maybe there's a silver lining in being poor.

I got a text from Blythe. She asked how I was doing. Um…*hello?!* You know what you put me through, bitch? She can't expect to just pick up where we left off before all this happened and pretend everything's forgiven. We're way past that. Part of me wants to talk to her and ask if she's responsible for this nightmare but the other part of me knows I should keep my distance.

Dan just texted me. He said, "We should meet." He must have driven straight home after seeing my mom. That's a long drive. I asked him where he wants to meet. He said the parking lot of St. Paddy's at 11:00pm. It's 9:30 now. St. Paddy's is the bar where we first met. Strange place to meet. Not *in* the bar. In the *parking lot*. I have this little voice in my head screaming, "Don't go!" But I have to. He's my friend and I need to know what's going on out of sheer, morbid curiosity.

Well, that was a letdown. Dan never showed up. I waited in that parking lot until 11:40 and he never came. Asshole. However, there was some guy standing a block away, staring at me for a couple minutes. It was freaking me out. When I started staring back at him, he left. It wasn't the same guy from my building. They had different body shapes. It definitely wasn't Dan. So I don't know if it was someone targeting me or just some weird homeless guy. I texted Dan to see what happened and he didn't respond. Big surprise. Whatever, I'm done with him. He can come back on his own if he wants. I'm through chasing him.

When I got home my notebook was on the coffee table. I'm pretty sure I remember leaving it on the couch. Not a huge deal, but it's something. Things have been pretty good the last few days. I don't want it starting up again.

KAREN'S STORY

I started messaging with an older lady named Karen. I think she's in her 70s. Maybe 80s. She said she has a ghost for a roommate. My first thought was: ok…*sure*. She said her husband died young, more than fifty years ago. After he died, she moved to a new house. She lives in England. She said the house she moved into was some sort of historical building. There's some caretaker guy from the Historical Society or whatever that comes by once in a while to check on it. When he first showed her the house, she says she saw an apparition of a woman in the back yard. This was the middle of the day, but Karen was shocked. The caretaker just said, "Oh, that's just the ghost. She's harmless." Just like it was the most normal thing in the world.

Karen says she's been living there for over fifty years and sees the ghost maybe two or three times a year. It happened more frequently when she first moved in, but it's slowed over time. She says the ghost is usually outside in the yard but has been seen in the house occasionally.

It never speaks or acknowledges her in any way. It just walks around. She says she'll see it for maybe five seconds at most. It will just appear, walk for a bit, then vanish into thin air. Karen said other than that, nothing scary or paranormal has happened in the house. She said it's a "lovely" house.

When I told her about my experiences, she suggested I move to England and live with her. She said, "Come live with me, dear. My ghost sounds much more friendly." Lol. Trust me, I'm tempted.

Karen was interesting to talk to and she was friendly, but she called me "dear" way too much. Maybe I'm being petty, but I don't like terms of endearment.

Karen's story is interesting in that her ghost is friendly. So I guess ghosts, like people, can choose to be good or bad. I'm pretty sure my ghost is bad. I just hope he's not *that* bad.

TUESDAY, DECEMBER 3, 2019

I was awoken this morning by a phone call. I got the job! Yay for me! (I just stood up to dance around in triumph). I start the day after tomorrow. Money problems, bye bye! Cooped up in this apartment 24/7, bye bye! New friends...*hopefully*. This seems like a new start.

Maybe this new event in my life will be enough to end the "activity." That Margaret woman said usually some sort of event starts it and some sort of event stops it. And it doesn't have to be anything major. What ended her haunting was her cousin moving in. Although I should mention this guy Tyler that I was talking to. He said his house was haunted and he moved with his friend into a new place and the haunting got worse. He said his friend was involved with drugs and stuff, so maybe it's because he had bad energy. It just goes to show these things don't make sense or follow any rules. But I guess I should just do as Addilyn said and stay positive.

This is how bad my social situation has gotten. I have this "friend" named Tamara. We weren't that close, but we were kind of friends when I started school. We haven't talked much the last year or so. Anyways, I wanted to go out and celebrate my new job. And to have some human contact. So I messaged her and asked if she wanted to go out tonight. She responded, saying she couldn't because she was "busy."

Then just now, I see a post from her on Facebook. She's at the bar with some people! She frickin went to the bar! That's what she meant by "busy." Why didn't she invite me? They couldn't let me tag along? Is there seriously something that wrong with me?

One of the guys at the table in the picture she posted was Mike, Blythe's ex, who we had the falling out over. He was sitting next to some blonde girl. Not sure if that's his new girlfriend or just someone sitting next to him. It's kind of a coincidence. I didn't know Mike and Tamara knew each other.

I was pissed off, so I commented on the post, "Looks like you're having fun." Maybe my sarcasm didn't register. She just clicked "like" on it. People are assholes.

I just did something I'm kind of ashamed of. There was a bunch of knocking in the apartment and it was annoying me, so I went out for a drive. I went up to Jasper Ave and found myself close to the bar Tamara and her friends were at. (No, I didn't subconsciously drive there to spy on them.) I parked nearby and I was contemplating going in to join them. What are they gonna do? Kick me out? I probably would have gone in if I'd had more money. I had to pay rent a couple days ago so I'm broke again.

I never got the chance to go in anyways, because after a couple minutes they came out. Tamara and the others walked away together. Mike and that blonde girl stood outside, talking. It looked like they were arguing before she finally stormed off. Mike sat down on a bench and looked really upset. I was tempted to go see what was wrong, but I didn't. He looked up and I thought he saw me, so I drove away.

I felt bad for my stalkerish behaviour, but it was also kind of fun. I feel bad for Mike. Why do girls always treat him bad? Maybe I should message him and see if he wants to hang out. Or is that just inviting more unnecessary drama into my life?

As I was driving home, there was a car on fire, parked on the side of the road. Two guys were standing there watching it. It was just engulfed in flames. That would be scary – you're driving along and your car starts on fire. I kept driving and soon passed a fire truck with its sirens on.

I stopped by the liquor store and bought a bottle of wine. I decided to celebrate myself without other members of the human race. Who needs 'em? Lol. I'm currently sitting here, enjoying it. And nobody is going to stop me.

Right as I typed that the lights flickered. I guess it's the friendly neighbourhood ghost reminding me of his presence. Fuck it. He can watch me drink. Nobody's going to ruin this for me.

WEDNESDAY, DECEMBER 4, 2019

Drinking a whole bottle of wine to yourself doesn't make you an alcoholic, does it? What if you give up using a glass after the second one and drink straight from the bottle? No? I'm good? Ok, good to know.

I texted my mom and asked if she'd heard from Dan again. I told her what happened with him pulling a no-show. She hasn't responded.

My car has been stolen! I went to the parking lot, and lo-and-behold, my parking spot is empty. I called the police and they said they'll be here as soon as they can. Awesome. I'm not sure if this is related to all the other weird stuff going on (people staring at me, coming to the house, etc.) or if it's just a random theft. I've never had a vehicle stolen before. I've never even had a vehicle broken into. It feels like a violation of my privacy. Some asshole's out there, driving around in my car.

The police officer just left. It took them six hours to show up. I guess they have more important things to do. He asked if I'd given a set of keys to anyone. Yeah, I give my car keys out to all of my friends! What a dumb question. I asked if they usually find stolen cars. He said, "Sometimes." I get the impression they won't do much to find it. If they come across it, they'll let me know, but what else can they do?

If they don't find my car by tomorrow, I guess I'm taking the bus to work my first day. It'll take more than a day for my insurance company to get me a rental. I hate taking the bus. Especially when it's crowded. You get the creepiest people on there. My new job's not that far away. I guess I could walk. It's probably only 45 minutes. Although it's winter so it'll be cold. What am I talking about? I'm not frickin walking! I want my damn car back!

They found my car. It was parked half a block away. I have no idea how it got there. All I can think is that it's my disembodied friend. But I'd have to see that to believe it. I had to go to the police station to sign some papers to get it back. The cop there was the same one who came by when I reported it. He looked at me like I was an idiot. I'm sure he thinks I parked the car there and forgot it. Which I didn't.

I did something tonight that I've never done before. I went to a movie by myself. Is that a weird thing to do? I don't see a lot of people going to movies alone. I guess there's nothing wrong with it. I just like going to movies with someone else. It's not really a group activity. I don't like going with a big group of people. I prefer to go with one person. Then after the movie you can go somewhere and discuss it. Dan was really good at that. We'd talk for hours about movies we watched, analyzing them and stuff. I miss him.

Blythe, on the other hand, sucked to watch movies with. She'd sit there and watch them, but after she'd just be like, "That was fucking stupid." Every damn time. She had a problem with every single movie we ever watched together. I don't think she's ever watched a movie she liked. Except Wizard of Oz. She loves that movie. Probably because there's a witch in it.

Anyways, I better go to bed. First day of work tomorrow!

THURSDAY, DECEMBER 5, 2019

Quick update before work. I thought I put my clothes in the basket last night before bed, but now they're lying on the floor. Again, I can't quite remember so I'm going to assume it was *me* that did it. It's been quite a while since there's been a major "incident" and I want to keep it that way.

Work was pretty good. It's always awkward the first day. You don't know anyone; you don't know where anything is. You pretty much feel useless. But it was ok. The people there seem nice.

I didn't want to be late, so I got there super early and had to stand outside waiting for half an hour because the building wasn't even open yet. Whatever. Shows I'm responsible.

Apparently bulldog man works out of a different office and was just there to do interviews, so I won't see him much. Doug. Dug.

They basically just had me fill out a bunch of stuff and go through the company policy manual and other formalities. Then they showed me around and I answered phones a bit and did some other stuff. Should be pretty easy. I have to work some weekends. But I get paid every second Friday. Maybe now that I have a regular income and some stability in my life, the bad stuff will just continue to go away until it's just a distant memory. Then I can finally have my life back.

This time it definitely wasn't me. I guess I spoke too soon earlier. I went to the store and when I came back, there was a stack of books, like seven high, on my coffee table. When I left, they were just scattered on the floor next to the couch. I guess the entity felt the need to pick them up and stack them. Not a huge thing, I just don't want the scary stuff starting up again.

Everything's going so well.

FRIDAY, DECEMBER 6, 2019

The fucking cops came back. Not about my car, not about Poe, but about that fucking murder! They were spouting off these people's names, asking if I knew them, which I *didn't*. I was like, "No, no, no, no," after every name. There was probably ten or twelve of them. The two moron detectives were looking at me like they though I was lying. One was like, "Are you *sure*?" "Yes, idiot, I'm sure!" (I didn't actually say that, but I thought it). They showed me a picture of some woman I'd never seen before and asked if I knew her. I didn't.

I flat out asked them what they think my involvement is. Like, am I a suspect in this murder? They were like, "No, your name just came up. These are routine questions." My name came up in a murder investigation?! From people I never met?! This is fucked up. Should I get a lawyer? Is someone making up shit about me?

I demanded to know who these people were. Were they also killed? Are they suspects? Should I be worried? I asked them if this has anything to do with the creepy guy in the hall. They said they didn't know anything about that.

Oh, yeah! They asked where I was yesterday afternoon! Luckily, I was at work, so I have at least a dozen alibis. I hope they don't call my work and ask. That'll look really good after my second day. Having the cops call to ask about my whereabouts. Fuck.

I still have this sneaking suspicion that Blythe is somehow involved with this. Maybe these people are some of her "witch" friends. Maybe they're after me and they killed some guy named Dale Bardem and the police got my name from Blythe. This is total speculation, but I have no other rational explanation. This is freaking me out worse than the ghost stuff. What if they accuse me of murder and I get arrested? I don't think I have the personality to do well in jail. If Blythe and her coven of witches are trying to frame me for something, I'm sure the police will see right through it. She's not smart enough to pull off something like that. I hope.

Maybe I should start keeping track of my movements in case I need an alibi. If the cops are like, "Where were you at 4pm on Monday?" I'll pull out my phone and say, "I left work at 4:30, stopped at Safeway, then drove home." Then they can check the security cameras at the store to confirm it.

I really hope they solve this murder soon so they can take me off their list of suspects. I'm tempted to tell them about Blythe, but if it's *not* her, I don't want to stir up that hornet's nest again.

I was on the couch, watching TV, when, I swear to fucking God, I heard a voice whisper, "Come here," from down the hall. This voice sounded female, but it was deep and raspy. Like an old lady. Really scary. After nearly having a heart attack, I worked up the courage to go down the hall to check it out. There was nothing there.

My shower curtain was closed and I tore it back, expecting something to jump out, but nothing did. It might have just been someone out in the hall, but I know in the pit of my stomach it wasn't.

Looks like it's back to the sleeping pills tonight.

SATURDAY, DECEMBER 7, 2019

This is a new one. I woke up this morning and I was backwards in bed! My head was where my feet usually are and vice versa. I probably just turned around in my sleep. But in all my life that's never happened before, so it seems weird to happen now. At least I slept.

Anyways, I'm heading out to work.

While I was on lunch break, I got a call from my mom. She left a message. I checked the message after I got off work and it was clearly a man's voice saying, "Hi, Genesis. Call me." More specifically, it was my *dad's* voice. I tried calling back but there was no answer and the mailbox was full.

Also, I don't know if I'm being paranoid, but I think the police are following me. When I left for work today there was a cop car parked up the street. When I got to work, there was one parked outside my work. I freaked out, thinking they were there to ask about me, but they weren't. I don't know what they were there for, but they never came inside. There are other businesses around that area, so maybe it had nothing to do with me at all. But I've been seeing them drive past all day. Maybe I'm only noticing because I'm paying attention to it now, but I've never seen this many cops around here.

The thing is, other than my job, I'm always alone. So if they accuse me of something, how do I prove it wasn't me? My alibi for every night is, "I was home alone." That's not going to make me look good.

On a positive note, I heard people at work talk about going for drinks last night. So that's cool if they hang out outside work. Hopefully I can join them and make new friends. This one guy, Oliver, seems pretty cool. His cubicle is close to the reception desk where I work. He's one of the programmers. I talked to him a bit on break.

Ugh. It's never-ending! I was sitting in the living room tonight and suddenly the power went out. The whole apartment was suddenly plunged into darkness. This would be terrifying enough in a normal situation but seeing as there's an evil entity stalking my apartment, it was a thousand times worse. I jumped up and tripped over the coffee table. I felt around for my phone and turned on the flashlight. It gave me some light, but somehow made it look scarier. I just ran for the front door. When I opened my front door, the bathroom door (which is right next to the front door) slammed shut. I'm not sure if it's because of the suction created from opening the door or if it was the ghost.

Usually when the power goes out, it goes out on the whole floor (or the whole building) but the lights were on the hall, so it looks like it's just my apartment. The fuse box is in the hall and I checked it. It wasn't the fuse.

While I was checking the fuse box, Mrs. Pearson came out of her apartment, on her way out. I asked if her power went out. She said it didn't and told me to call emergency maintenance.

Before I could call them, the power went back on. I went back inside and sat there, scared that it would shut off again. I lit a bunch of candles, just in case. There's nothing creepier than sitting in a haunted apartment, surrounded by candles, power or not. Lol. Jesus.

Now that I think about it – where was Mrs. Pearson going? It's 1:30 in the morning. She was dressed like she was going out on a date or something. She must have a more exciting life than me.

SUNDAY, DECEMBER 8, 2019

I set my laptop on the coffee table and left it recording all day while I was at work to see if I could catch anything on camera again. I checked it when I got home and about ten minutes in, the little boy pokes his head out from behind the couch! Only for a split second, but I paused it and you can clearly see his face. I'm almost positive it's the same boy I saw crawling in the hallway before. WTF?!

I sent the clip to Addilyn to get her opinion but I don't expect to hear back. People really like ignoring me, don't they? I'm going to record more tomorrow.

I wonder if I could make money posting these videos online. I doubt it. People would probably just accuse me of faking them.

More craziness. I looked out my bedroom window shortly before sunset and there was a guy standing on that little patch of grass next to the visitor parking where I saw the creepy little girl. It looked like he was staring up at my apartment. There are lots of apartments in this building, but given recent events, I assumed he was looking at me. In a momentary lapse of judgement, I decided to wave at him, which was a huge mistake. The second I waved he started walking towards the building. I got this chill up my spine. I knew he was coming up here.

I quickly lost sight of him as he approached the building. I ran to the front door and watched through the peephole. Technically, you have to be buzzed into the building, but with so many people coming and going it's easy for someone to let you in. I stood there with my eye glued to the peephole for a few minutes. Just when I'd given up and figured the guy must be a resident, he rounded the corner at the end of the hall, marched right up to my door and started pounding. I hid in the bathroom and called the police. The guy kept pounding for a few minutes. I could hear him talking but couldn't make out what he was saying.

Of course, he was gone by the time the police got here. I had to give a statement. I've had more dealings with the police in the last month than I've had in my entire life. They checked around the neighbourhood but couldn't find him. I told them about the other guy in the hall. They said they'd check with building security to get the details on that one. So in the end, once again, there's nothing I can do except call them if the guy comes back.

Like, seriously, is this paranormal?! They look real enough. Are the little boy and girl *ghosts* and the older guys *real*? Or are they all ghosts? What the fuck is going on? Remember, kids - if you see a creepy guy staring at you, don't wave at him.

JOEL'S STORY

This guy named Joel commented on a post and something about him intrigued me, so I messaged him and we ended up chatting.

He lives in Los Angeles. He told me his ordeal started after he dropped out of college (sound familiar?) and the visits from what he calls "The Man in the Checkered Shirt" began. This man in a plaid, red and black checkered shirt would appear in his room in the middle of the night. He wouldn't say anything, he would just stand there, staring at Joel. Usually, he was in the corner of the room, near the door, but sometimes he'd move around. After it happened a few times, Joel said he'd sleep with his phone nearby and try to get a picture of the man. But the pictures never turned out. They'd either show nothing at all, a blur or an "orb" (another common paranormal phenomenon I don't put much credence in). He sent me a couple of these pictures and I didn't see anything abnormal about them. Sometimes pictures have weird lights or reflections in them. Doesn't mean it's paranormal.

However, Joel seems very genuine and a lot of what he said is similar to my story. That being said, my first reaction to his story was extreme skepticism. It's kind of strange that in this #metoo era, we're still slow to believe someone's story. I think people are generally honest, but when someone tells you something that's hard to believe, your first thought is, "You're full of shit." Why should it be up to a person to prove their honesty? Why can't we just believe people as a natural reaction?

Of course, the flip side of this is that a lot of people lie about this kind of thing. At least I think they do. Some of the stories I've read are just way too "out there" to be real. All the stuff about reptilian aliens secretly controlling the government and stuff like that…

Even though I've gone through similar things recently, I still had a hard time believing Joel (or any of the others I've spoken with). It took a while, getting to know them, before I decided they were "worthy" of my trust.

Anyways, back to Joel's story. Joel says the man in the checkered shirt (whom I'll call The Man for simplicity's sake) never said anything, but he could hear him breathing. I asked for more details on what he looked like and Joel said sometimes he wore a hat and sometimes he didn't. He said he couldn't really make out facial features, other than eyes, but he got the impression The Man was "old." He said the body could only be described as a black shadow with a clear human outline. He said the eyes alternated between three colours – glowing red, glowing white and black. Blacker that the black shadow of his face.

He said the only thing that had colour to it was the red in the checkered shirt. And even that was a very dark red. I asked what kind of pants or shoes he wore and Joel said he either couldn't remember or never noticed. (Must have been hard for him to look away from the glowing eyes.)

Joel said the first couple times The Man appeared, he ran from the room in terror. The second time it happened The Man was standing by the door and when Joel opened the door to run out, he felt resistance as the door passed through The Man's body. He said it was like trying to force open a door against a strong wind.

The third time it happened Joel said he sat up in bed and flicked on the light. As soon as the light came on, The Man was gone. This definitely supports the idea that it was in his head but keep reading. The next time it happened Joel said he sat up in bed but didn't flick on the light. He just sat there, staring at The Man. He said The Man didn't overtly do anything to threaten him, but there was definitely a malevolent feeling about him. I guess you could say that about any stranger that enters your room in the middle of the night without your consent. It was at this point that Joel grabbed his phone and took several pictures, but none of them showed anything concrete. He asked what it wanted, but it didn't reply. He told it to leave, but it just stood there, staring. Joel even said, "Leave, in the name of Jesus Christ," but it didn't move.

It was there for another minute or so, then it was gone. This is interesting. Joel said it didn't "leave," it was just suddenly not there anymore and it took him a moment to realize that. He said it was hard to explain.

The next time it happened, he flicked on the light again but The Man did not disappear. He still couldn't make out the features, though. The Man was still a dark mass in a human shape with a checkered shirt and freaky eyes. This time he teleported. He was standing in one corner of the room, then suddenly he was in another spot.

Joel says that even though he was terrified every time this happened, he was still able to keep a lid on his fears and think rationally. He said his main thoughts were, "Is this really happening?" and, "What is this thing?"

I've read about shadow people (so had Joel) so we both concluded that that's what this thing was. Funny enough, we even read other stories about people seeing "The

Man in the Checkered Shirt." Most of the people who saw him did so before they ever heard of him, so it's not like they hallucinated something they read about.

I asked what kind of hat he wore the times he wore one. Joel said once it was a "Charlie Chaplin" hat, the other time was an "Abraham Lincoln" hat.

Joel said he saw The Man a few times after that but he didn't stay as long. More like a brief glimpse.

I asked Joel if he'd seen ghosts or anything else before this point. He said throughout his life he'd seen some weird stuff like UFOs and lights in the sky. He thought he saw a ghost on a family trip England when he was eight. His whole family was there but their mom insisted it was just a person they saw. Joel and his older sister stick to their story that it was a ghost.

Joel says it was about this time (after the last sighting of The Man) that his life began to unravel. His aunt died and his mom was diagnosed with cancer a few days apart. Then his boyfriend of two years broke up with him without warning. His friends started acting weird and distanced themselves from him for seemingly no reason.

This seems like what's happening to me. I wonder if there's something subconscious going on, like a negative vibe people going through this project that repels people.

Joel said he lost his job at a restaurant because someone accused him of stealing food, even though he didn't. I'm taking him at his word for this, I really don't know him that well, but I'll give him the benefit of the doubt that he's not a thief.

Just like me, the more weird shit that happened and the more people distanced themselves, the more he turned inward, which just led to a downward spiral of madness. And, just like me, he felt he had nobody to turn to.

It's funny - if you have a drinking, drug or gambling problem, there's so much help available. If you're a victim of crime, there's organizations to help with that. If you're going through a haunting…you're alone. Nobody will listen except other people who have gone through similar things. It's like we're forming our own little support group of misfits outside the norms of society.

The next thing that happened to Joel is the strange text messages. He'd get random messages from strangers that said everything from, "Hi," or "What are you doing?" to nonsensical things like, "Cosmopolitan heartbeat," "Toxic sexuality," "Assassins' Pen." Weird stuff like that. He read me a whole list of messages that all came from different numbers. Those are the only ones I can remember off the top of my head. After a couple weeks of this, they got more threatening, saying things like, "I will kill you," and "You will burn."

He said if they were all from the same number he would have gone to the police because it would have been the work of a single person. However, since it was always a different number, he knew it was paranormal-fueled and there was nothing the police could (or would) do. He said he had a feeling in the pit of his stomach that getting the police involved would make it worse.

At this point in our Skype conversation, Joel got emotional. He looked like he was about to cry. He asked if we could talk later and I said sure. He called me back forty-five minutes later and apologized. (Why do people feel the need to apologize for crying?) So we resumed our conversation. On a side-note, Joel was the only person I actually chatted with "face-to-face." Everyone else was just email and messaging. But I trusted Joel more.

Joel said the next thing that happened was that he began hearing voices. At first it was just a word or two at random times, but it grew into short sentences. He said usually it sounded "American" but sometimes it switched between Irish and Scottish (very strange).

When it started, it would call him "Danton" for some reason. I asked if there was a significance to that name and he said no. He joked that maybe the ghost had the wrong person at first. One day it switched to calling him "Joel" and began giving him specific instructions. Instead of just random phrases with no meaning, the voice would say things pertinent to the situation. If he was talking to someone, it would say, "Punch him!" or "Burn it!" or some horrible statement.

After a while, it became more persistent, shouting at him. This led to awkward encounters where he'd be in public or talking to someone and this voice in his head would be screaming at him, making it impossible to have a conversation. People would give him weird looks and it was just another reason for him not to go out in public.

Joel has a neighbour named Reginald and the voice started telling him to kill Reginald. Eventually, the voices were replaced by an overwhelming compulsion to carry out the act. The voices ceased all together, but he had this intensely strong desire to strangle or stab Reginald to death then bury his body in his yard.

At this point in my conversation with Joel, I began wondering what I'd gotten myself into. He assured me he wasn't going to do it. I suggested he get professional help and that made him angry. He said, "You think I never thought of that?!" Apparently, he went to a psychiatrist or counselor but they said they couldn't help him. WTF? He said he told them what was going on (leaving out the stuff about wanting to commit murder) and the guy was like, "Sorry, I can't treat you." Is that even legal? Aren't these people there to help those in his situation?

Joel said he decided to keep it to himself and try to "wait out the storm." He moved to a different house and that seemed to help a bit. But he said his life had long since "turned negative." Everything he tried was a failure and everything that could go wrong *did*. He went on some disastrous dates. He'd lose things – his keys, his credit cards. His car got dented by a hit-and-run driver. He got a new job only to have the company go out of business a week later. The house he used to live in burned down after the new owner fell asleep with a lit cigarette.

Joel said he felt so alone he started thinking of suicide. But he had this feeling that one day it would be ok. This shit can't last forever, right? (something I think all the time). He decided to join paranormal groups on social media to see what other people were saying. He didn't post or comment for a long time because he didn't want to risk being rejected by the last possible group of people on Earth who might be willing to take him seriously. Eventually he commented on a post and hinted at his own story. This is when I replied to his comment and we started our own chat then agreed to Skype.

Apparently, I'm the first person other than the counselor he's told about this. He seemed grateful that I was willing to hear him out. He said just telling someone who didn't reject him was a weight off his shoulders. It makes me feel good that I was able to help.

I told him my story too and he was a sympathetic ear. Just like it was for Joel, it was great to get the whole story out. Sometimes if feels good to open up to a virtual stranger. They have less reason to judge and there's less of a downside if they do react negatively. You can block them and never speak to them again.

I just wanted to share Joel's story with you. Something about him made me feel a connection.

TUESDAY, DECEMBER 10, 2019

Another scary episode last night. I woke up in the middle of the night and just had this chill up my spine. It wasn't cold, it was something else. Like that electric feeling again. I instantly new something paranormal was happening. I was scared to look around my room. I just *knew* I was going to see something standing there. (Man in the checkered shirt, perhaps?) But I had to look. There was nothing in my room, but I could see a pair of feet under the crack in the door. Something or someone was standing in the hall outside my room. I just froze and stared. The light in the hall was on and all I could see was the shadow of feet there. They were shuffling around, moving back and forth, then after a little bit they stopped and stood there. I held my breath, hoping they'd go away.

I assumed it was the ghost due to the way it was shuffling back and forth. The movement just seemed too weird for a human. In a way, I was glad it was a ghost. If it was a human, like a man in my apartment, it could have gone much worse. It was still scary as hell through.

I wanted to say something to see if it would react (and hopefully leave) but I was terrified it would burst into the room and jump on me.

Then it walked away. It took me another ten minutes before I worked up the courage to go out and look. My heart was racing.

I opened my door and peeked out. Nothing there, so I went out to my living room/kitchen area and flicked on the light. Nothing there either. I made my way down the hall towards the front door/bathroom. I could still feel that tingling feeling, like the hair standing up on my neck. I knew the thing was still there. I went into the bathroom and couldn't see anything but the shower curtain was partially closed. I instantly knew the thing was standing behind it but I *had* to look. I *had* to see it. It felt like I was in a horror movie. I reached out, threw back the curtain and… (dramatic pause) …there was nothing there. At least nothing I could see. (I'm keeping my shower curtain open from now on so this doesn't happen anymore.) The tingling feeling was still there, but it suddenly vanished in a suction of air that I could feel blow through my hair. It wasn't like something moved past (or through) me, it was like the act of it disappearing caused a vacuum. As soon as it was gone the energy in the room was different. I could feel it was no longer there.

That didn't mean I was less scared though. The whole thing had me traumatized. I knew I wouldn't sleep so I put on coffee and stayed up all night watching movies. Thank God for comedies. I can't stand horror now.

This is kind of a side-note, but when I'm scared, I like to watch movies I've seen before. Usually ones I've seen many times. It gives me comfort. Watching a new movie is a new experience. You have to pay attention and you're not sure what you're in for. With a familiar movie, there's comfort in knowing what's coming up. And if the movie is good, I'll usually notice little things I never noticed before. It's similar to how you listen to your favourite songs over and over again.

The worst feeling in the world is being unable to sleep and knowing you have to work in the morning. After being scared to the very pit of my soul because of the entity in my home, the next worst feeling is *that*. I spent the whole night checking the time on my phone. "Three more hours until I have to be at work," "Two more hours until I have to be at work." Ugh.

I debated calling in sick, but I'm still new so I don't think it's a good idea. Plus, I always feel guilty calling in sick. I know they think I'm lying. (In the past when I've called in sick it was because I was hungover, so I guess I *was* lying).

I went to work and put in a full day even though I was pretty much a zombie. I drank lots of coffee and tried to be chipper, but it was a struggle.

I did talk with Oliver some more. That was definitely the highlight of the day. He's quite a bit older than me. Mid-30s probably. But he's super nice and fun. And I can't exactly be picky with my friends at this point. I invited him over to watch a movie tomorrow night. I would have invited him tonight but the only thing I thought of all day was rushing home to jump into bed and sleep until morning.

In case anyone reading this thinks I have a romantic interest in Oliver, I don't. I don't think he has romantic feelings for me either. At least I haven't picked up on any of the signs. I just want to be friends with him. It's horrible to say, but I need a replacement for Dan.

WEDNESDAY, DECEMBER 11, 2019

After work yesterday, I came straight home, took off my jacket and shoes, went to my room, hopped into bed and went to sleep. I couldn't care less about any ghost, I just needed to sleep. It was the best sleep I've had in a long time. I slept for thirteen hours and woke up today feeling great. If anything paranormal happened during the night, I was in no position to know about it.

I left my laptop recording in the living room yesterday, but it doesn't look like I captured anything on video. At least nothing I noticed quickly scrolling through it. I'll watch it in more detail later.

When I left for work today there was something going down on the street outside my building. A cab had stopped on the side of the road and the driver was pulling some guy out of the back. They were both yelling at each other. The guy getting pulled out was drunk (pretty sure). The cab driver dragged the guy out onto the median then got in his cab and drove off. Of course, this was on 122 street, which is a busy street. Even after the cab was out of sight, the drunk guy was still yelling, "Fuck you!" from the middle of the street. People were honking and the guy was giving them the finger. He started wandering around in the middle of the street with cars honking and trying to get around him. Eventually, he crossed the street, walked through the church parking lot and disappeared.

I watched all this from the parking lot before getting into my car. I hate it when stuff like this happens. This neighbourhood is usually really nice. Definitely the safest I've ever lived in. But bad stuff can happen anywhere.

I debated calling the police on the guy, but I'd prefer to limit my interactions with the police, so I didn't bother. Hopefully someone else did.

Work was much more bearable today seeing as I didn't have to struggle to keep my eyes open. My boss is kind of a jerk. His name's Don. I don't like him. He treats me like I'm the lowest form of life at the office. I know I'm just a lowly receptionist and I'm new, but you can still treat people as equals. On Wednesdays they buy donuts for everyone. I went to the break room to fill up my coffee (which is allowed. People do it several times per day) and I grabbed a donut on the way out. Don saw and he's like, "Donuts are for on your break only." WTF? It's not like I was standing there, eating it. I was taking it back to my desk. No company time wasted. What a jerk. Oliver doesn't like him either. I doubt anyone likes him.

Speaking of Oliver, he's coming over tonight. I'm kind of nervous about it. It's not a date in any way, but I'm so anxious to make a new friend it feels like a job interview or something. I have to put on a show and make sure he likes me so he'll hang out with me in the future. Yes, I know it's ridiculous, but that's how I feel.

The return of Ghost Girl! I wanted to see if any of those creepy guys were coming to my door in the middle of the day, so I taped my tablet to the front door with the camera pointing through the peephole. It gave a perfect shot of the hallway outside my door.

After work, I quickly scrolled through the footage to see if I could see anything. I saw a quick flash of something and backed the video up to see what it was. It was the same damn ghost girl that I saw outside. For some reason I want to call her "Texas Tammy," but I'll stick with Ghost Girl. She crawled around the corner by the elevators, up to my door, knocked, then crawled away.

I wish these ghost kids' parents would make them behave. And stay the hell away from my apartment.

So what's the next step? First, she was in Texas, then she was outside my building, now she's outside my door. Will she be *in* my apartment next? She's slightly scarier that the little boy, but neither of them are that scary. The little boy being in my apartment honestly doesn't scare me as much as it should. It's the grown man entity

that's really frightening.

I'm tempted to reach out to that kid in Texas and tell him I believe him now. I've

seen that little girl myself. But he's really young and I don't want his parents finding

out about our conversation and having them think I'm trying to warp their child by

feeding into his paranormal delusions.

Oliver should be here any minute. I hate having to "host" people for the first time.

Like, am I supposed to serve drinks and snacks? What do people expect of me? When

I go to someone's house, I don't expect them to wait on me like a butler. I'm pretty

chill. They can offer me a drink if they have one, but I don't expect much else.

Growing up, whenever we had company coming over, Mom would go into freak-

out mode and make us clean the house top to bottom. Even the basement and places

people never went. And it was always a big deal that we keep our bedroom doors

closed. Seriously, Mom, if the people you're having over are that judgemental, you

should find new friends. It's your alcoholic buddies coming over, not the fricking

Queen of England.

My dad hated it too, but he knew better than to argue. He'd say, "Well, the house

needs to be cleaned anyways. May as well do it now." When I was really little, my

mom would make me change into different clothes when she had friends over. Like I had to dress up a little. I'd be five and she'd say, "Terry and Sandra will be here soon, go put on your (whatever clothing she thought would impress them the most)." As I got older, she stopped doing that.

It was worse if it was somebody coming over for the first time. Then the house had to be fucking immaculate. As she got to know people better, she let her standards slip a little. If it was just the neighbours coming over, all we had to do was tidy up.

This is kind of off-topic, but I don't remember playing with the neighbourhood kids much growing up. We lived in a house on a normal residential street. There were lots of other kids my age, but I never played with them. I can't remember why. Not sure if there was a reason for it, or if I just didn't like them. I had other friends, but we'd always have to drive to their house, or they'd come to us because they lived farther away. In elementary school, one of my best friends was named Tara-Lynn and I remember it was always such a big deal for the two of us to play together because it involved parents of one child having to drive to the other. Mom was always like, "Tara-Lynn lives so far away. You should find friends who live closer." Now that I'm older and drive, I realize it was really only a 15 or 20 minute drive away.

I wonder what ever happened to Tara-Lynn. She moved away before Jr. High and I never heard from her again. I tried looking her up online but can't find her.

Anyways, back on topic – I did clean a little before Oliver came over. I bought some pop for us. I didn't think getting alcohol involved our first time together would be a good idea. I really hope this goes well.

Ok, that went as horribly as it possibly could have gone. We watched a movie then we were sitting around talking for a couple hours. Everything was going fine. Oliver is cool. He's had such an interesting life. I was being charming (and hopefully interesting too). Then Oliver got up to go to the bathroom and came out acting all flustered. He's like, "I gotta go. I work in the morning." I could tell something was wrong, like he was scared. That's a poor excuse to leave suddenly. We both work at the same time at the same place. This was only 11pm. I asked if everything was ok and he said it was, he just had to go. He was in such a rush to get out of here, he didn't even put his jacket on. He just grabbed it and left without tying his shoes. I went to the window and saw him run across the parking lot to his car.

I don't know what happened, but I suspect the ghost scared him somehow. Something must have happened to him in the bathroom. "Thanks, ghost! You just scared away my best shot at a new friend!"

It's going to be awkward at work tomorrow. Maybe I'll ask him about it again. But if it was something paranormal that happened to him, how do I explain that? "Oh, *that*? That's just the ghost haunting my apartment. By the way, we should be friends!" I feel like I have a contagious disease. Who will want to come over and be my friend when they have a ghost tormenting them?

Hopefully I can patch things up with Oliver. There's always the chance we can be friends but just never hang out at my place. He better not tell anyone at the office what happened. I don't want to be known as the weird girl with a haunted house.

Maybe the paranormal "doubt" will work in my favour this time. Maybe after a day or two he'll start to question if he really heard or saw what he thinks he did.

Around 1:00am, as I was getting ready to go to bed, a heard this loud "boom" in the living room. I went to investigate but didn't see anything abnormal. It's possible it came from the apartment next door.

THURSDAY, DECEMBER 12, 2019

I didn't sleep too well last night. Too scared. During the day, it's easy to rationalize this whole thing and think, "It's not that bad. It can't hurt me." But as soon as it comes time to turn out the light and go to sleep, all the fear comes back. I managed to sleep a bit but not enough. I need to get more sleeping pills. I think I'll make an appointment with the doctor to see if I can get stuff stronger than the over-the-counter kind.

More scariness. I got out of the shower this morning and "DEI" was written on the bathroom mirror, like someone used their finger to write in the steam. That's pretty disturbing. If it can do that, it means it has a definite physical presence. It's also unnerving that it's in the bathroom while I'm showering naked two feet away. Pervy ghost was probably watching me. I don't know what "dei" is supposed to mean. I Googled it but couldn't find anything. Is it trying to say, "Die," but it's just a really shitty speller? There's definitely something threatening about it.

Oliver was being weird all day. I said hi in the morning and he just said hi and walked away without looking at me or saying anything else. Usually he'll stop by my desk during the day to chat but today he didn't. I can see his workstation from my desk and one time I saw him just sitting there, staring at the ground, doing nothing for several minutes. Don walked by and asked what he was doing, so he started working again. I really think the ghost did something to him. I just don't want to ask him what. I'll just leave him alone. He can come to me when he's ready.

But I think it's a good idea if I don't have anyone over until this mess is dealt with.

I really like my new job. Not just because the job is decent, but because I feel safe. Nothing paranormal seems to happen outside my apartment so I have a good 8 or 9 hours when I can not be scared and live like a normal person. It's bright in the office and the people are nice (for the most part). I notice it towards the end of the day. I start dreading having to go home. When I leave work, I'm always looking for an excuse not to go straight home. Usually I'll stop by the mall and walk around, checking out stores for a while. I walk by that clothing store and sometimes I see Erin in there, but I never go in. I'm worried about bumping into her while walking around.

Today, I stopped by the mall to postpone having to go home. When I eventually came out, there was a police car parked next to me. It wasn't there when I went in. Probably just a coincidence, but you never know.

I nearly freaked out because a dog in a truck started barking, but it kept barking at other people after I pulled out, so it wasn't directed at me.

I saw something out of the corner of my eye run under the couch tonight. It looked like a rat. I don't see how that's possible since there are no rats in Alberta. Which is definitely a good thing, but I almost prefer rats to cockroaches. At least they're mammals and have fur. Insects are the worst thing ever. Rats are almost cute. Does that make me weird? Don't get me wrong, I still don't want them in my house. But anything is better than roaches. Or bed bugs. Bed bugs are pretty much the worst insect you can get. Blythe had them in her old apartment. They multiply so fast and are nearly impossible to get rid of. And they feed on you, that's the worst part. At least roaches are not out to get you, but bed bugs are. Blythe would show me the blankets on her bed and there'd be little blood marks all over it from where she killed them. She'd wake up and they'd be crawling all over her and the bed, so she'd squish them and blood with come out. Her blood.

Apparently, bed bugs are coming back in a huge way. It's like an epidemic. I heard they were big in the middle ages but went away and are making a return. Exterminators are backed up trying to deal with them so there's a waiting list. It took a month before they could come to Blythe's building and exterminate them. And even then, they had to come three separate times over several weeks. And each time she had to wash all her clothes and sheets and tie them up in bags, then empty out all her closets, cupboard and storage spaces so they could spray. It was a big ordeal.

Someone on the internet said having bed bugs is the worst thing to happen in life short of losing a limb. That's probably an exaggeration but having them sucks. After seeing what Blythe went through, I never want them in my apartment. Although I'd rather have them than what's currently "living" in my apartment because at least bed bugs can be exterminated.

Anyways, back to the story. I swear I saw a rat or some little, furry thing scurry under the couch, but when I looked there was nothing there. I don't want to tell the landlord about it because there's a chance it's a ghostly apparition and I don't want to cause an uproar. If I see it again and confirm it's real, I'll tell them. If not, I'll chalk it up to being some of the usual spooky shit.

Before I went to work today, I taped my tablet to my peephole again. I just watched the video. I didn't see any weird guys, or Ghost Girl, but I did see something strange. Mrs. Pearson got off the elevator and went to her apartment, but suddenly stopped and turned to look at my door. She creeped up the hall to my door, like she was trying to be quiet. It looked like she was straining to listen to something inside. She seemed spooked. Then she walked quickly back to her apartment and went inside.

Very strange. I don't know what to make of it. I don't want to say anything because she might find it weird that I was recording her. I didn't hear any noise on the video, so I don't know what she could have been hearing.

I have no reason not to like Mrs. Pearson, but something about her angers me. It's been like that since I first met her. I don't know why. It's not normal to detest someone for no reason. Maybe "detest" is too strong of a weird. There's just something about her I don't like. Don't get me wrong, I can be civil. But I don't think I could ever be friends with her. Something about the way she talks makes me angry. And she's always apologizing, which irks the hell out of me. If I'm on the elevator and she catches the door as it's closing, she's always like, "Sorry, sorry. So sorry, Genesis." Like the extra two seconds is going to ruin my day. We get off on the same floor anyways. Why does she have to be so submissive? Not every situation requires an apology.

I was in my room tonight when the cutlery drawer in the kitchen opened on its own again. It's not that big of a deal. It's at the bottom of the "scariness" scale. Funny how I've become so desensitized to some of this stuff that it no longer bothers me. A few months ago, a drawer opening on its own scared me to death. Now I'm like, "Oh, it's just the ghost." It takes more to freak me out. Voices, feeling that presence - those things scare me. Opening and closing doors and drawers is kid's stuff now.

Something else happened tonight that isn't so much scary as it is annoying. I came into my room and my bedsheets had been pulled off the bed. That better not happen in the middle of the night while I'm sleeping. That would scare the shit out of me. This is more of a nuisance. I hate making the bed. Now if it could do the laundry for me…lol

It got worse tonight. WAY worse. It was close to bedtime and I walked into my room and saw this freaky-looking old lady floating outside my window! I kid you not! She looked like the frickin witch from Snow White or something. She was wearing a black dress and just floated there, staring at me with this evil-looking smile. I'm on the 13th floor remember. Her eyes were fucking scary as hell. I ran out of the apartment in my bare feet (not a fun thing to do in December in Canada). When I got outside, I looked up at my apartment and there was nobody up there. People outside were probably like, "What's this crazy barefoot chick doing out here?"

I would have stayed outside longer because I was so scared, but my feet were freezing, so I went back inside. Talk about trepidation going back to my apartment. I was so scared she was inside, waiting for me. But I looked around and she wasn't there. There was a mark on my bedroom window, though. Like a fog mark from someone breathing on it from the outside. Maybe that was there before, I don't know, but that woman was definitely there. No doubt in my mind.

I'm sleeping on the couch tonight and keeping the blinds closed. I'm also going to record the living room window on my laptop all night to see if I capture anything.

FRIDAY, DECEMBER 13, 2019

I was late for work this morning and I got in shit from Don. I didn't fall asleep until five this morning and I forgot to set my alarm. For some reason the old lady incident scared me more than seeing the shadow of someone walking around my house. When I saw that thing under my door, it had no face to it. Seeing an actual, malevolent face makes it a thousand times worse.

Maybe the person I saw at my bedroom door *is* the old lady? I don't think it was. I'm not sure why, but I just got this vibe that the person I saw under the door was male. Not that it matters, it's just my perception of it.

I hid under several blankets last night on the couch. I was scared to look at the window in case that woman was floating there again. I'm going to watch the video now and see if I can see anything. My blinds are thin black cloth, so even if they're closed, I'll be able to see if someone was on the other side.

I went though the whole video and didn't see anything. I made a drawing of her though. I haven't drawn in a while. I felt good to draw. I miss it. Anyways, I'm going to have a shower and go to bed. Try to sleep. I'm so tired.

I saw Oliver and Don arguing at work today. They were in the conference room with the door closed so I couldn't hear them, but I could see them through the window. Oliver was all upset and it looked like Don was trying to calm him down. I don't know what they were talking about, but Oliver looked really frazzled. He's usually quiet and reserved.

Oh, my God, it's getting worse! I was in the shower and all of a sudden, a hand pushed on the shower curtain and touched me. I could feel its fingers! What the fuck?! I opened the curtains and there was nobody there (of freaking course).

This changes everything. It touched me! If it can touch me, it can hurt me.

I think it's time I called a priest. I've been in denial, hoping it would get better, thinking, "It's not that bad." But I have to face reality. It's getting worse. Like the thing is getting stronger. At first it could just move things, then it started talking, now it's touching me. What's going to happen next? I don't even want to imagine.

MONDAY, DECEMBER 16, 2019

I finally got to see Dan.

Although, not under the circumstances I would have liked. I was in my room last night when I heard the deadbolt on my front door unlock. Then I heard the door open, close, and somebody walking down the hall towards my bedroom. You can imagine how scared I was. I was beyond petrified. I went out and there was Dan, coming down the hall at me with his arms stretched out like freakin Frankenstein or something. I screamed, thinking he was attacking me, but instead he just gave me a hug. A big long hug. He had this sadness in his eyes that killed me to see. Then he just turned around and walked out. I followed him out to the elevator, trying to talk to him, but he never said a word. He got on the elevator and held out his hand so stop me from following him. And that was it. He left. No closure or anything. I guess there's nothing more I can do for him. Dan was my best friend and that guy who came into my apartment last night was not the Dan I know. So sad.

A while back I gave Dan keys to my apartment in case of emergency. That's how he got in. I guess he was too messed up to realize a text or a knock at the door to let someone know you're there was more appropriate than just letting yourself in.

Dan and I were such good friends. It seems like this is the end. This is worse than anything else I've gone through. I can only hope he'll be ok.

This happened last night. The combination of fright and being tired was too much. I couldn't write in my journal in that state. So I just went to bed. I slept ok. Nothing paranormal. That I know of.

I drove past Dan's house today and there were people moving in. So I guess he doesn't live there anymore.

I talked to the landlord and they're going to change my locks tomorrow. As much as I love Dan, I don't want him returning in his current state.

This has me wondering if it was Dan who left the hair/twig voodoo thing in my storage closet. Dan had keys, Blythe didn't. But then again, Dan was acting normal when all this started and Blythe was harassing me, so I don't see what his motive would be.

I'm considering reaching out to Blythe to see if she wants to meet up. I haven't decided yet.

There was a weird mark on my wall today. It was dark brown. It looked like a smeared handprint. It was some sort of grainy substance. I couldn't tell what it was. It didn't have a smell and it wiped off fairly easily. Another example of this thing taking physical form, I guess.

I've been completely fucking paranoid about taking a shower since that hand tried to grab me. I shower with the curtain open and just jump in and out as quickly as possible. I'm so scared it's going to grab me again.

TUESDAY, DECEMBER 17, 2019

The escalation continues. I woke up this morning and found my big kitchen knife on my bed! I take this as a threat. If it can bring this into my room while I'm asleep, what's to stop it from stabbing me?

I did it. I texted Blythe and asked if she wants to meet up. I instantly regretted it the second I hit send, but it's too late now. Things can't exactly get worse. (Knock on wood).

Blythe messaged me back and said she wants to meet up too. She's on her way over. This should be interesting.

That actually went quite well. Maybe it's because I'm lonely, but it was really good to see her. I think she felt the same. Just being in the same room with her made me feel better.

One of the first things she said was, "Your apartment's haunted, isn't it?" I said it was and she said hers is too. Turns out it *was* her that put that hair thing in my closet. She said she snuck in when I went downstairs to the laundry room. She got my hair when I crashed at her place after we were out partying one night. That was quite a while ago, so I couldn't understand why she needed my hair then. She said a lot of the black magic stuff she was into involved hair, so she just wanted a sample of hair from people she knew. It's not only for negative purposes. It can be used for good too. (Either way, kind of creepy, Blythe.)

She said she was so mad at me and wanted to put a curse on me. Ted, that guy from the séance we went to, told her how to do it. She said she didn't really expect it to work, she just did it to make herself feel better. (That's Blythe for you). Supposedly, leaving this stupid thing made of twigs and hair in someone's home after saying a Latin chant unleashes a demon on them. But Blythe thinks she did it wrong because the demon is haunting her too. Like it backfired.

I told her I was communicating with it and it said it wasn't a demon. She said it lies.

I suggested she contact this Ted guy and ask him how to stop it. But apparently, he committed suicide by hanging himself from a pipe in his parents' basement. So no chance of that happening.

The scary thing is that it scratched her. She showed me these scratches that look like claw marks on her arm. Very scary. She said it called her name a few times but hasn't touched her other than the scratches.

We compared our haunting stories and it felt great to get this off my chest to another person. It's more personal (and meaningful) with a friend than it was with Joel over Skype. (No offence Joel.) It's comforting that she's going through the same thing. It's like I have someone on my side now.

She said she sometimes burns sage and that makes it stop for a bit but it always comes back.

We even talked about moving in together. Maybe that way we can face this thing together. And also split the rent.

Some of the freaky shit she went though is really interesting. She said one time her entity stacked a bunch of plates on a chair in her living room. What is it with ghosts and dishes? Hers also likes playing the piano. Blythe has two pianos in her apartment.

One that the previous renters left behind and one that's hers. She keeps one in the living room and one in the spare bedroom. She said they'll play on their own. One will play and when she goes to investigate, it will stop, and the other starts playing. She says it always plays on the high keys, never the low. And it actually plays little melodies, not just random notes. I guess that's a huge sign of intelligence – being able to compose music. Although I guess there's no proof it's actually writing what it plays. They could be existing songs Blythe has never heard before.

She also thinks she saw a gnome in her apartment. I felt bad because I laughed when she told me that. She saw it run by out of the corner of her eye. She went to look for it but it kept running around, just out of sight. It made this high-pitched, "tee-hee," sound. It ran into the bathroom and slammed the door. She went in to look and there was nothing there. She said she never got a good look at it, only through her periphery. She said, "It wasn't that scary. It was only two feet tall. I could just kick it." Lol. Oh, Blythe, you can be so funny.

We discussed whether or not it was the same entity in both our apartments. Blythe thinks it is, but I'm not so sure. Hers seems different. It does different stuff. But there are similarities. Blythe's ghost seems to have spoken out loud more, but she never communicated with it like I did.

In hindsight, I should have forgiven Blythe sooner and reached out to her. She apologized for everything. She said she feels terrible, she just overreacts when she's angry because she feels everything so passionately. Not sure if I buy that excuse, but it feels good to have her back in my life. She's back to being the old Blythe, no longer going through that weird phase. She said the haunting pushed her to give up all the witchcraft and black magic.

I told Blythe I was thinking about calling a priest to bless the house. She said I could try, but it might make it worse. I've been hearing that too. I'm just prepared to try anything. She thinks a blessing might not be enough. We might need full-on exorcism. Of course, that makes it worse sometimes too, according to what we've been reading.

I told Blythe about Dan and Oliver. She said it's possible the demon is haunting them now too. It might have attached itself to them just because they were in my house. (I wonder if it's the same for that pizza guy who came here a few weeks back).

I feel really bad now. I didn't do it on purpose, but if Dan and Oliver are going through hell because of me…that's terrible. I guess Blythe and I shouldn't have anybody into our apartments until this is dealt with.

I forgot about Addilyn. She came into my apartment too. Maybe *she's* haunted now and that's why she's ignored me since she came over. And the building handyman too. Jeepers, I might have spread this to a lot of people.

I guess I can still call a priest. The demon couldn't haunt the priest, right? Don't they have some sort of "powers"? I'm not religious and don't really believe in that stuff. I'm (pretty much) an atheist. But I didn't believe in demons up until now. I think it's worth having a priest over. If he does become haunted, I'm sure the Catholic Church has the resources to help him.

Blythe left and we agreed to hang out again soon. I feel so much better! I have a friend again!

I worked up the nerve and called a priest. The whole thing scares me for some reason. Something about the Catholic Church is so creepy. I think it's the clothing and the rituals and the Latin and the crucifixes and the imagery. It's just unnerving to me. I don't see how people can be inspired by it. Those Southern U.S. Baptist churches, I could see how people find that uplifting! If I had to go to church, that's the kind I'd go to.

It's also the bad shit the Catholic Church has been involved in. The persecutions throughout history, the corruption and sexual abuse scandals of recent times. I'm not sure if all that has been dealt with (you don't see it in the news much anymore), but it's still at the forefront of my mind.

But I guess I have to give them the benefit of the doubt. I'm willing to forget the past if they can give this fucking demon out of my house so I can have some peace.

I was worried they'd think I was crazy so I didn't tell them about the haunting, I just said I wanted to have my house cleansed. They asked if I was a member of the church. I said I wasn't, but that I was thinking of joining (I lied). They said they'd see who was available and get back to me.

The man I spoke to, although polite, sounded old and grumpy. Exactly how I'd pictured him.

My mom finally called me. Not to say hi or check to see if I'm ok, but to yell at me because the police came to her house asking questions about me! She lives in Thunder Bay, Ontario. The other side of the country. So the Edmonton police must have contacted the Thunder Bay police to inquire about me. What could they possibly want with me out there? Is it something to do with Dan since he went out there? Or is it something to do with the murder they've been talking to me about? It doesn't make sense. My mom would barely give me any details. She said they didn't mention a crime, they just wanted to know about my background and when she last talked to me and all this other stuff. God knows what she told them.

My mom was like, "Genesis, what have you gotten yourself involved in? Are you hanging around with bad people again?" *Again?!* She tells people I used to hang out with a bad crowd because one time in grade 11 she saw me standing with some people and one of them was smoking. She equates that to me being a drug addict, hanging around with murderers. She's the biggest hypocrite ever. I smoked one cigarette in high school and I didn't like it. I haven't smoked since. I drink sometimes, but I don't do heavy drugs. I smoke weed once in a while, but not that much. I was hardly a "bad kid."

Oh, my God! More *mom* drama! She called back saying some guy was banging on her door. She was like, "Was he a friend of yours?" No, he's not a friend of mine! I live in frickin Edmonton in case you forgot!

She said, "Well, *Dan* came to see me." I told her don't even pretend I had anything to do with that. She won't even tell me what Dan was doing there, so how can I know anything about it? Dan's trip out there is their little secret. It's got nothing to do with me. She was like, "Don't yell at me, Genesis. I've had a rough day!" Yeah, sitting around drinking all afternoon must be exhausting. I actually said that to her. Needless to say, she wasn't pleased.

She said it's strange that the police were there, now some guy's pounding on the door. I have to admit she has a point. And there were those guys coming to *my* apartment. Is it related somehow? I have no idea. Maybe it's someone looking for Dan? This whole thing is one big mystery. But I'm more concerned with preserving my own sanity and getting this thing out of my apartment than dealing with any larger issues.

What really pissed me off was when she said, "Are you sure it's not some friend of yours?" I said, "I don't have any friends." She said, "What a surprise." I was so pissed off I just hung up on her.

WEDNESDAY, DECEMBER 18, 2019

Oliver was being downright bizarre today. I saw him walking around swatting at something like there was a wasp buzzing around him. He looked paranoid like he was on drugs. Very weird. People were staring at him, wondering what he was doing. He saw people watching and just stormed off. That was half-way through the afternoon and he never came back.

I ate five donuts at work today. I'm not a big junk food eater, but for some reason I just craved donuts today. You got a problem with that?! (Just kidding, if anybody is actually reading this, I love you!) I'm not sure why this seemed important enough to mention, but I thought it might be amusing. Maybe I can make donut day my goal-reaching day. How many donuts can Genesis eat in one day? Each week I'll eat one more. Then, a year from now, I'll be eating 52 in a day! Man, I'm so dumb sometimes. lol

I got an email from Joel, that guy I was talking to who had urges to kill his former neighbour. He said he was arrested and is out on bail because he broke into that neighbour's house and attacked him. *Oh, my fricking God!* He said he'd never actually do it. He told me he wasn't going to kill him, he just needed to "release the anger." I was firm with him and told him he needs to tell the police or the prosecutor or whoever that he has mental issues and needs to see a psychiatrist. If a judge orders it, then I'm sure the psychiatrist will take him seriously. I also asked him not to contact me anymore. I'm dealing with too much of my own shit. He agreed. I hope he gets help and doesn't eventually kill that guy. Or anyone else. It's really too bad. I liked Joel.

I hope I don't end up going down that path.

I heard back from the church. They said Father Leonard can come over tomorrow at one. I don't know if that's his first or last name. I'm not sure how it all works. I don't know much about the Catholic Church (or any church for that matter) so I don't know what to expect. Most of my knowledge comes from TV shows and movies. Most notably, the Exorcist.

I just hope it works and he's able to drive this entity out. I'm sure they bless lots of houses. He'll just think it's routine. My hope is that the general "house blessing" will be enough to get rid of it.

It feels weird having a priest come to the house. I can't put my finger on why. It makes me uncomfortable somehow. Probably because of my preconceptions of the church I mentioned earlier. I feel the same about going to the dentist. But they both need to be done, so I guess I'll put my feelings aside and go through with it. It'll be worth it if it works.

Christmas is coming up next week and something tells me I'll be spending it alone. Right when I wrote that last line the cutlery drawer in the kitchen opened on its own. My first thought was, "I guess I won't be spending Christmas "totally" alone."

I went to the grocery store and when I got back a bunch of spoons and forks were arranged around the drain in the kitchen sink, kind of like the marks on a clock. There were eight of them. The sink was empty when I left so I guess the ghost took them out of the drawer. Pretty tame compared to other things that happened, but noteworthy none-the-less.

I might have to move from wine to hard liquor to sleep at night. The wine's not hitting me as hard as I need. And, yes, I know you're not supposed to mix alcohol with sleeping pills, but I'm at the point of desperation.

And anybody reading this better not call me a hypocrite for bashing my mom's drinking then doing it myself. This is *way* different. I have a good reason and I don't have kids to take care of. I know I've mentioned that before, but it bears repeating. Plus, I'm drunk right now.

More knocking on the wall tonight. More aggressive than normal, like it wanted me to answer, but I ignored it. It can't tell me what to do. It doesn't control me.

THURSDAY, DECEMBER 19, 2019

Oliver is in even worse shape now. This afternoon I went to the break room and he was sitting on the floor, leaning against the wall. He looked homeless, like a drug addict. He was unshaven and wasn't wearing a shirt and tie like he usually does. He didn't even look at me when I walked in. He just stared off into space with a glazed look in his eyes. Something about it scared me so I didn't say anything to him. I went and found Don and told him. He told me to get back to work and he'd deal with it. I really hope Oliver is ok.

The priest came over on my lunch break today. It was pretty quick and uneventful. The priest was way younger than I was expecting. I thought it would be an old man. Again, probably just my TV/film bias. He just walked around sprinkling holy water and saying some prayer. When he started, we heard this laughing. He looked at me and I told him it was the people next door. It wasn't.

When he was finished, he left without so much as friendly chit-chat. So I guess now I sit back and wait to see if it works.

I was thinking about my dad today and how much I miss him. I thought about the time he took me fishing. I was 11. We were living in Calgary and we drove to the mountains to fish in a lake there. Just the two of us. I relished the alone time I had with Dad. My childhood was dominated by an overbearing mother so it was rare Dad and I could just sit together and talk. Mom was always home and Dad was gone for work so much.

This one time we had a whole day together. I think Mom was supposed to come, but they had a fight and she backed out. *Good.*

We saw a dead deer on the side of the road that had been hit by a car. I remember being angry with the faceless driver who hit the deer. I sat there in the front seat, refusing to speak, angry at the injustice the poor deer experienced. My dad said it wasn't the driver's fault. It's just part of nature. I couldn't understand that. Getting nailed by a car and left on the side of the road is part of nature?

That incident aside, it was an amazing trip. I loved every second of it. I knew I had limited time with my dad (I didn't know *how* limited at the time. He died less than a year later), so I seized the opportunity and told him everything. We sat there in the boat we rented, out on the lake, and I talked non-stop for several hours. I was almost afraid to stop and take a breath for fear my mother would show up and interrupt our time together. After I'd run out of things to talk about, I realized the reason we were there to begin with. To fish. Neither of us had caught a single one. We weren't even really trying. I felt bad. My dad said not to worry. Fishing wasn't important to him. But I was. Fishing was just something the two of us could do together. He also said I was turning into a "very interesting young lady," which I took as the hugest compliment ever. On Monday at school, I told my best friend Tara-Lynn that "people" had been saying I'm an "interesting young lady." She was like, "I'm interesting too!" She was jealous.

We stayed out on the lake for quite a while. The sun was starting to set and, in my mind, I thought if it went below the mountain tops, it would be too late to drive home. Dad and I would have to rent a tent and sleep outside. I wanted this so bad.

But it was not to be. As it got darker, Dad said the dreaded words, "Well, we better get heading back." I wish that day could have lasted forever. Neither of us caught a fish, but that wasn't the point.

The drive home was depressing. It started raining. I didn't feel like talking. There was nothing to look forward to when we got home. I asked Dad if we could go fishing again the next weekend. He said, "We'll see." We never did.

We got home and my mom started yelling at Dad the second we walked through the door. I just went to my room and listened to music. After she finished berating

Dad, she came and pounded on my door, yelling at me for something or other. All I could think was, "I wish it was just me and Dad."

Little did I know that later that year it would just be me and *Mom*.

When Dad died, I was so mad at him. I know that's ridiculous, but at the time I couldn't believe he was cruel enough to leave me alone with Mom.

Anyways, it felt important to write that memory down. I talk about my mom way too much in this journal. Dad was way more important to me so he deserves some page time.

This is weird. It's 10:00pm right now and the church just called to ask if Father Leonard came over today. Apparently, he left to come to my place but never returned. I told them he came and went this afternoon. I'm not sure what to think of this. I'm worried he's gone missing and I was the last person to see him. That shines the suspect spotlight directly on me. And I already have the cops poking around about another murder. Last thing I need is them coming by to ask me about the priest. Or worse, going to my mom.

FRIDAY, DECEMBER 20, 2019

Oliver quit today. No word, no goodbye. This guy Dan (not my Dan) came to my desk and said, "Oliver just quit." I looked up to see Oliver crossing the office floor and storming out the door. I guess that's the end of that saga. I can't help but feel guilty. I'm almost positive the demon in my apartment did something to him.

My worst fears were just realized. The police came by my apartment asking about the priest. Apparently, he still hasn't been found. It was two different detectives this time. They must think I'm some psycho killer by now.

I asked them if this is linked to that other murder. They said they didn't know, that wasn't their case. That's a lie. Like these cops don't talk to each other. They didn't accuse me or anything but I was sick of police coming by asking questions. I told them flat out, "I didn't kill the priest, I didn't kill that Dale Bardem guy, I didn't kill anyone." They looked at me like they were surprised. In hindsight, flipping out like that is probably what guilty people do, but I just snapped. I even said, "You want to talk to me again, talk to my lawyer." Of course I can't afford a lawyer, but it felt good to put my foot down.

I told them to leave and they left. Yes, I kicked two cops out of my apartment! Lol. Now I'm sitting here, worried they're coming back with the tactical team to bust my door down and arrest me.

I hung out with Blythe again tonight. It was fun. We went to the bar for a bit. She paid for my drinks. I don't know where she gets her money, she's not working either. Afterwards, we walked home. It was warm out for December. We sat in the park behind some school and smoked a joint. I hadn't gotten high in a long time. It felt good to hang out with her again. Just like old times.

She said when she woke up this morning and tried to open her bedroom door, it wouldn't open. It was stuck shut. She'd given up and was about to crawl out her window (she's in a basement apartment) when the door suddenly opened on its own. She walked out and said, "Thanks," and heard a voice that sounded like, "Mmm hmm," like it was agreeing with her. Strange.

Blythe said she's started abusing her demon. Calling it names and putting it down. "You're so stupid," and stuff like that. If a door slams, she'll say, "So lame," or something. She says the activity seems to have slowed since she's been doing that. She thinks she's shaming it and its embarrassed to make its presence known.

We agreed we should try not to talk about the haunting stuff. When it seems like it's taking over your life, sometimes you just want to have a normal conversation with a friend. Not just talk about how you're scared to be in your own home and you fear for your life.

I told her I was keeping this journal to help me process everything that's happening. She said she might do the same.

It's almost back to normal with us. It's like the hell between us the last couple months was a dream. Like it never actually happened.

Blythe said some girl's been coming by her apartment and knocking on her door. It's her ex, Mike's, new girlfriend, June. Blythe hasn't been answering the door because she doesn't know what June wants. It must have something to do with Mike. June was outside Blythe's building today and Blythe had to go through the alley so she wouldn't be seen.

June must be that girl I saw arguing with Mike outside the bar that time. Blythe did say she was blonde.

SATURDAY, DECEMBER 21, 2019

I woke up this morning to find, "No more prist," written on my laptop. On the very word document in which I'm writing this. Very unnerving. Thinking back, I shouldn't have deleted it. I should have kept it as part of my journal so anyone reading this could have seen an actual typed message from a demon.

I'm not sure if it meant, "The priest is no more," as in he's dead, or if it means, "Don't bring another priest over." I'm leaning towards the second explanation.

Kind of freaky that it can communicate through my laptop now. I was tempted to write back to it but I'm not supposed to communicate.

And once again, it's a shitty speller.

Things have gotten about as worse as they can get. I was sitting on my bed, putting on a pair of socks when I felt a hand grab my ankle. It came out from underneath the bed. Talk about the freakiest fucking thing that could happen. Jesus Christ.

I ran out of the apartment and walked around for a few hours until I got too cold. Then I came back. I sat on the couch, with my feet tucked up under me.

Lesson learned: priests don't work.

I don't know what I'm going to do now. I'm out of options for getting rid of it.

I got a hold of Blythe and told her what happened. I know we agreed to limit our discussions on it, but this is too much. She came over and hung out with me. I felt much better with her here.

We stayed up talking all night until the sun rose. I feel like I can handle this if she's around. We're really talking about moving in together. It would make these events easier to cope with if there was someone else in the house. Especially someone who believed me.

Blythe said June came back today and she finally let her in, just to see what she wanted. She was worried June would attack her but she's actually really nice. Apparently, June is concerned because Mike is acting really strange but won't tell her what's going on. June asked Blythe if she did something to him (which would have been my first thought too, knowing the way Blythe can be). Of course Blythe hadn't talked to Mike in quite a while.

June told her scary stuff was happening at Mike's house and they think it's haunted. So they've been staying at June's place but stuff started happening there too, even when Mike wasn't around.

Blythe told her the same thing has been happening to her. They compared stories and Blythe said June felt better now that somebody else was around that believes what she's going through.

Wow, this thing is sure spreading. Blythe gave it to Mike, who gave it June. Blythe also gave it to me. I think I passed it on to Dan and Oliver and maybe other people. It's spreading like an STI. If it keeps going like this, the whole city will be infected soon. What if it keeps spreading and goes world-wide?

Blythe sure knows how to cause problems.

SUNDAY, DECEMBER 22, 2019

I called in sick at work today. Blythe and I were up talking until half an hour before I was supposed to be at work. I hadn't slept or showered or anything. I just don't think I could have handled a day of work on top of everything else. Blythe left and I'm going to try to sleep. Nothing paranormal has happened since the ankle-grabbing last night. But it's no great feat that nothing has happened in one 12-hour-period.

I took my mattress off the frame and moved the frame to my storage closet. Now my mattress is directly on the floor. No room for anything to hide under the bed and grab me. I'm going to sleep on the couch anyways. It's daytime so it's not as scary.

Great news! I've been fired! Not because I called in sick, but because the fucking police went there asking about me! Don called me and said, "I don't know what's going on in your personal life, but we can't have that kind of thing going on here." Wow, thanks police! Get me fired when I didn't do anything wrong. Merry fucking Christmas!

Is it possible to sue the police for doing that? Or my job for letting me go for a bullshit reason? This can't be legal. I didn't do anything.

My whole world is falling apart. I don't think there's a way out. I'm pretty drunk as I write this. Maybe it does run in the family. Whatever. Even if I am an alcoholic, at least I'm not a huge bitch like some other people (Mom). I'm taking two sleeping pills tonight. That should knock me right out. The ghost can touch me all it wants. I won't even notice.

I'm listening to gospel music. Maybe that will keep it at bay. I don't normally listen to gospel, but it's nice. It's peaceful and uplifting. Maybe ten years from now I'll be known as the crazy lady who lives alone and listens to gospel music.

Oh, Genesis, where did you go wrong in life?

I considered staying in a motel, but that's not a long term plan. Even if I stayed there for the night, I still have to come home and face my apartment sooner or later. And I'm really low on money. With no job, it's going to be hard. I don't want to wind up homeless.

I wonder how bad it is being homeless. There are thousands of homeless people in Edmonton, so it can't be that bad. I just wonder if it's preferable to living here with this invisible thing fucking with me. It might be ok to be homeless in L.A. or somewhere warm, but Edmonton is so frickin cold half the year.

Hard to believe I'm in the position where being homeless is an attractive alternative.

Hey! Don't judge me!

MONDAY, DECEMBER 23, 2019

I'm hungover. My head hurts. I think one sleeping pill is enough. Especially if I'm drunk too.

More developments in this ongoing drama. I was watching the news and someone was arrested for killing that Dale Bardem guy. They showed his picture. It's the guy that I saw out in the parking lot, staring at my apartment! The one who came and banged on my door! In a way this is good because it takes the suspicion off me. But at the same time, how am I mixed up in all this?

Some guy I don't know kills some other guy I don't know, comes to my fucking house banging on the door and gets me fired because the cops go to my work asking questions. I don't know if I'll ever find out what's going on. I just hope this is the end of it. I don't want those fucking cops coming to my house again. Or going to see anyone I know.

I hope they don't call me to be a witness or anything. I don't see why they would. I don't know anything.

TUESDAY, DECEMBER 24, 2019

I burned some sage that Blythe gave me. She said sometimes that makes the ghost go away for a while. I burned it right before bed. I decided to face my fears and sleep in my bed. Big mistake.

Even with the sleeping pill and being half-drunk I was awoken in the middle of the night by banging and scratching on my bedroom door, like something was trying to claw its way in. It was growling like a vicious dog. I yelled, "Poe, if that's your spirit, go away! You're being a bad boy!" It stopped. I got up to go look but as a I reached for my doorknob it started again, even worse. I went and sat on my bed, listening and crying as it continued for the next hour.

I tried texting Blythe, but she didn't answer. Probably asleep.

It's Christmas Eve. This is supposed to be a happy time but it's anything but for me. I wish I had someone to spend Christmas with. Blythe is spending it with her dad and sister. She invited me but I politely declined. I wanted to go, but her dad creeps me out. He's never done or said anything bad to me, there's just something about him I don't like. He's been to jail for theft and things like that. He's not a bad guy, but he's not a good guy either. I see a lot of Blythe in him. Anyways, I don't think I would have enjoyed it. It would be awkward, like I'm an outsider. I've never met Blythe's sister. She's never really talked about her.

I wonder if it's true the demon follows you if you move. I've certainly read about enough cases where it was. And that's what everyone seems to be saying. But, of course, every case is different. I wonder if there's a distance you can move where it won't follow. I read somewhere it can't follow you over a body of water. That's hard in Canada since the entire country, and the U.S., is connected by land. The entire western hemisphere is connected. So I'd have to move overseas to get away. That's just not possible. And I don't even know if it's true. I'd hate to uproot my life, move to Australia, just to find the fucking thing followed me.

Or maybe I could take Karen up on her offer and move to England.

WEDNESDAY, DECEMBER 25, 2019

Merry Christmas!

I woke up this morning with scratch marks on my stomach. Five of them. Not deep, not bleeding, but definitely there. I assume it has something to do with the demon dog outside my door last night, but I can't be sure. Aren't demon scratches supposed to come in threes? Or is that just in the movies?

I feel in real physical danger now. First it was grabbing me, now it's scratching me. If it keeps getting worse, what's going to happen? How far will this thing go?

I hate that I can't see any sort of bright future. I used to think it would pass or I could learn to live with it. But now it seems like there's no way out. This will never end. I'll have to die to find peace. Really scary to think about. Especially on Christmas.

This is the first Christmas I've spent alone. The last couple years, my mom flew back and stayed with me. I doubt she'll even *call* this year. I could try calling *her*, but she's supposed to be the mature one. She wants to talk to me, she can call.

Everyone else is with their families, opening presents and being happy, while I'm sitting here putting cream on demon scratches and worrying it will attack me any second.

I went out for a walk. The streets are deserted. It's weird. It's like some snow-covered post-apocalyptic movie. I went to the store and bought a cake. That's my Christmas present/dinner for myself.

I called Blythe to wish her Merry Christmas. She's miserable. I guess she doesn't get along well with her family. She said, "We should have just spent Christmas together." My feelings exactly! Next year, that's what we'll do. If I'm not killed by this demon first.

We decided we're definitely going to move in together asap. We looked on the internet for places and found a few that might work. We emailed them. It's going to be hard since neither of us are working. I don't think they'll let us move in without reasonable means to pay the rent. So we're both going to start looking for work tomorrow. We can help each other out. It would be great if we could work at the same place.

It's kind of exciting. Even if the demon follows us, it's still cool to be living somewhere new. Blythe is talking to people from her old (witch-related) social circle to ask about getting rid of it. Hopefully it will be a thing of the past soon. But I've stopped expecting that. I'm prepared for it to last forever. I just don't want to get my hopes up anymore. Nothing kills the soul like constant disappointment.

THURSDAY, DECEMBER 26, 2019

Boxing Day! I remember when I was a kid, Boxing Day was second only to Christmas Day. You got to spend the whole day playing with all your new toys. It was so wonderful. I miss being a kid. I wish I could be 11 forever! Being an adult ruins everything.

TREVOR'S STORY

Trevor is stupid. Just want to get that out of the way before I tell you this ridiculous story. We both commented on somebody's post on a paranormal page and he PM'd me. He seemed normal so I messaged back and forth with him.

Then he told me the "Bigfoot story." He said he watched a movie about bigfoot. Then the next day, he was out walking and *saw* a bigfoot. This was the first red flag. You see a bigfoot the day after watching a bigfoot movie? *Riiiiiiight.*

Also, he lives in New York. Manhattan to be specific. This isn't the deep wilderness, it's one of the biggest cities in the world. Was this bigfoot walking down the street in downtown Manhattan? I guess they have Central Park, but I still don't believe it.

He said the sight of it scared him, so he ran. But over the next few days, he kept seeing it, always closer and closer to his home. Eventually, he saw it directly outside his apartment building.

The next day, he says it started talking to him (it speaks English apparently). It told him it was sent from another dimension (!) to bring Trevor an important message. But it couldn't give him the message right now. It had to wait until the right time.

So the bigfoot has been living with him for the last few weeks, waiting to give him the message. (Sigh.)

I played along and asked if he could take a picture of the bigfoot and send it to me. He said he tried, but the bigfoot doesn't appear on camera. Of course it doesn't, Trevor! (sarcasm level: extreme).

My last message before deleting and blocking him was, "Make sure it pays its share of the rent." There are so many problems with this story, it's not worth getting into. I doubt anyone reading this believes it any more than I do. But it really makes me angry. Some of us are *actually* going through hard times with paranormal shit and struggle to have people believe us. Then idiots like Trevor make up stories, tell them publicly and cast doubt on all of us. Why do people lie like that?

I really debated whether or not to include that story in this journal. The other ones are conceivably true. At least the people seem genuine. I just thought it was interesting. However, if I hear of a guy in New York and his bigfoot roommate, I'll be the first to admit I'm wrong.

Maybe there's a movie idea in there somewhere. I'd have to buy the story rights from Trevor, though. And I'd rather never speak to him again. What a weird guy.

I went out for a walk today and I said, "Merry Christmas," to every person I saw. Even though I'm a day late, nobody seemed to mind. I just felt like spreading Christmas cheer and being happy, even if it was forced. Everyone smiled and said it back to me, so that was good.

Of course, as soon as I was back in my apartment, the feeling of dread returned.

I spent the rest of the night watching some of my DVDs with the directors' commentary turned on.

FRIDAY, DECEMBER 27, 2019

Blythe is dead!

SATURDAY, DECEMBER 28, 2019

Blythe's sister posted it on Facebook yesterday. That's how I found out. She said they don't know what happened yet. It's being investigated and the family wants privacy, so I don't want to message them with questions.

This better not lead back to me. If the fucking cops come by asking questions, I won't even let them in the house. I'll just say, "I have nothing to do with it. If you think I did it, arrest me, otherwise fuck off!"

This is a nightmare. We mended our friendship and were supposed to move in together. She was my only friend. Now I'm truly, utterly alone.

I know you're all thinking it and so am I, so I'll come out and say it: did the demon kill Blythe? I can't see her committing suicide. At least not now that everything was going so well. Not under these circumstances. We had future plans. She wouldn't do that to herself without any notice.

This can't be happening. I think I'm still in shock. Like it's going to turn out to be a mistake. Or a cruel prank.

Oh, Blythe, why did you have to go?

Someone just posted on Karen from England's page that she died today. What the hell is going on? It said she died peacefully of natural causes. Karen was old and she died happy, so I guess there's no reason to grieve over that. But Blythe was 21 and in good health. There's nothing natural about that.

I guess whoever moves into Karen's house next is in for a big surprise!

Given what's happened, I made a decision. I'm going to try communicating with the demon. There's no way it can worse. Maybe if I talk to it, I can find out what it wants and get it to leave. I have to do it. And it looks like I'm doing it alone.

It finally hit me. Blythe is really gone. Forever. I spent the whole day crying. I'm not even sure what to write. It seems like I should say something, but what do I say? I guess I'll just say this:

Blythe, I love you.

This communication thing is harder than I thought. It's not responding to the knocks. I tried to write to it on my laptop but got no response. I tried using the bathroom mirror after a shower but got nothing either. I'm hesitant about using the mirror because I don't want it anywhere in the vicinity of the bathroom. But the other part of me doesn't give a fuck.

I considered using a Ouija board but they're hard to find. I found some on Amazon, but they're too expensive. I tried making one out of construction paper and a planchette made from twigs and paper, but it didn't work. I'm not sure if it's the best method though. I heard Ouija boards cause bad things to happen. But at the same time (all together now!), how can it get worse?

I don't get it. It's communicated with me before, using those same methods. I've heard it speak on more than one occasion, so why won't it work now? Can it only communicate *sometimes*? Or just when it wants to? I don't know how it works. I don't know "the rules."

I'll keep trying. Maybe I just have to wait until it reaches out to me. Nothing scary has happened since Blythe died. I'm not even going to entertain the thought that it's over. I know it's not. Maybe it's just resting. Waiting.

I'll do anything to get rid of it. I'll fucking kill someone if I have to. Probably not. But I'm that desperate.

MONDAY, DECEMBER 30, 2019

My cross was taken away. I've been wearing it nonstop since I bought it. I was wearing it last night when I fell asleep on the couch but when I woke up, it was gone. I guess the demon made it disintegrate into thin air. No big loss. It wasn't much help anyways.

I miss Blythe so much. I wish we'd never had our stupid fight. Maybe things would have turned out differently. At the very least, I would have had more time to spend with her.

I'm totally excited now! The knocking started and I knocked back. It took a few minutes, but it finally started responding. It's really weird how it works. You need to form a rhythm with it. At first, I'll knock and it will knock back 15 or 20 seconds later. It's not in the same pattern or number I did, so it's hard to tell if it's responding or just knocking randomly to be annoying. But I'll knock again and it will respond sooner. I'll keep that up until it's knocking back instantly. But usually it's still random. So I'll start imitating it. If it knocks three times fast, I'll do the same. If it knocks twice, slowly, I'll do the same. Then I'll start repeating the same knock over and over again until *it* starts copying *me*. Sometimes it takes a while, but it eventually works.

Sometimes I have to repeat that whole process over and over because it won't "click" with me. It will just stay random and I'll get bored or pissed off and give up. But I just got it working. Now it's answering questions I ask out loud again.

I also figured out a way to communicate with it beyond just a yes or no. You'll see how in the following conversation. (Sometimes I'm just so smart! Lol)

Here's the conversation (once again, one knock is yes, two is no):

Me: Are you still there? (Yes)

Will you answer my questions? (Yes)

Is today Friday? (No)

Is today Monday (Yes)

Are you mad I brought a priest here? (Yes)

If I agree never to bring a priest over again, will you leave me alone? (No)

Ok, then, I'll invite a priest over again. (There was a flurry of rapid knocks)

You don't want me to do that? (No)

Then leave me alone. (No)

You're not being reasonable. (Yes)

Do priests scare you? (No)

Then why don't you like them? (This wasn't a yes or no question so it didn't answer)

Can a priest hurt you? (No)

Can they get rid of you? (No)

I'm not sure if it's telling the truth or not. Some of what it says doesn't make sense or seems to contradict what it said earlier.

The conversation continues:

Me: Do you hate priests? (Yes).

That priest that came to my apartment, Father Leonard – is he dead? (Yes)

Did you kill him? (No)

Was he murdered? (Yes)

Did you have something to do with my friend Blythe's death? (No)

Were you haunting her too? (Yes)

Was she murdered? (No)

Did she kill herself? (There was no answer)

Did you hear me? (Yes)

Did Blythe kill herself? (Still no answer)

Are you refusing to answer the question? (Yes)

Fine. Did you do something to scare that guy, Oliver, who came over? (Yes)

Did you do something to scare Dan? (Yes. And this answer wasn't a knock. It was more of a loud pounding like someone hitting the wall with their fist. It made me jump. Maybe it really didn't like Dan for some reason)

Me: Was that one knock, meaning yes? (Yes)

I want to talk to you and I need your answers to be more than a yes or no. Is there a way to do that? (Yes)

How? Can you write on my laptop? (No)

How about on the bathroom mirror? (No)

But wasn't it you who wrote to me on those things before? (Yes)

So why can't you do it again? You can only do it sometimes? (Yes)

You can't do it now? (Yes) (This got me excited for a second)

You CAN do it now? (No)

Can you use paper? (No)

Well, you're pretty useless then, aren't you? (Yes)

But there is a way to communicate with you more than yes or no? (Yes)

Is it something in this apartment? (Yes)

Writing on the wall? (No)

At this point, it hit me!

What if I ask you a question and you respond with knocks? One for "A," two for "B," three for, "C," etc.? Would that work? (Yes)

I could barely contain my excitement. I grabbed a pen and notebook from my room and ran back to the couch. I'm asking it questions now, but it's a very long process. It's slow to answer and many of the answers don't make sense. And it takes a long time to count out letters of the alphabet.

This will probably take all night, so I'll just write down the answers then update this journal with my findings tomorrow.

Goodnight, everybody reading this! Hope you have a great night's sleep while I'm talking to a demon!

TUESDAY, DECEMBER 31ˢᵗ, 2019

I was up all night talking to the demon. Then I slept all day so it's nighttime again now. Good way to mess up my sleep pattern, but it was totally worth it. It was actually pretty cool.

This is the conversation. If you're wondering why it's not very "in depth" remember it had to spell out words with knocks, so even a short word could require counting over a hundred frickin knocks. I wish I knew Morse code. Anyways, this is what I got:

Me: What is my name? (This was a test question to see if it would work)

Demon: Ien.

Me: I-E-N. That doesn't make sense.

There was a series of ten knocks, which is "J."

Me: "J"? Are you trying to say "Jen"?

There was one knock meaning, "yes."

I told him that was a "good job." Not sure why. He's not a puppy. I told him I usually spell the short form of my name, "G-E-N," but I'm not going to be picky here.

Me: What is your name?

Demon: Cyr.

Me: Cyr? That's your name? (One knock for yes)

I got out my phone and tried seeing if I could find anything about a demon named Cyr but couldn't find anything. From this point on, I'll call him Cyr instead of "demon." I pronounce it like "sear," by the way. Like you sear a steak.

Me: I just looked up your name and didn't find anything. I guess you don't have a social media handle. (Damn, I'm hilarious) (He didn't answer this, by the way. I guess he doesn't appreciate my sense of humour).

Me: Why are you haunting me?

Cyr: I need you.

Me: What do you mean exactly?

Cyr: Don't know.

As a side note – talking to "Cyr" was frustrating. He had a hard time answering questions that were even the slightest bit difficult. Like ones that took thought. I had to keep things simple and his answers were even more simple. It was like having a conversation with a two-year-old.

Me: Why did you pick me?

Cyr: You pick.

Me: I picked me?

Cyr: Well.

Me: I don't know what that means. (No answer)

Me: Cyr? I'm not sure what you mean by "well."

Cyr: Proptic.

Me: That's not a real word. (I looked it up to check).

Cyr: Hard.

Me: You find this hard?

Cyr: (One knocks for yes)

Me: I asked why you picked me.

Cyr: You pick.

Me: That's what you said last time. I'm not sure what that means. Do you mean I picked myself? Or do you mean I was picked?

Cyr: (Two knocks)

Me: Does that mean "no." Or does that mean you're indicating the second choice?

Cyr: (Two knocks)

Me: Are you choosing the second choice – that I was *picked*?

Cyr: (One knock)

You see how frustrating this can be, just getting an answer to a simple question?

Me: Are you haunting me because of that thing Blythe left with my hair on it?

Cyr: (One knock)

Me: Why does that thing make you come after me?

Cyr: I know.

Me: You know what?

Cyr: Don't know.

Me: You meant to say, "I don't know."

Cyr: (One knock)

Me: How long will you keep haunting me?

Cyr: Eternal.

I think that answer is pretty straight-forward.

Me: Are you a person who used to be alive?

Cyr: Falling.

Me: What does that mean?

Cyr: Comcal.

Me: I'm not sure what that means either, Cyr. Can you clarify?

Cyr: Unsur.

Me: Are you a human who used to be alive? Knock once for yes, twice for no.

Cyr: (Two knocks)

Me: How old are you?

Cyr: (Twenty-six knocks)

Me: You're 26-years-old?

Cyr: No. (He spelled this, no knocks).

Me: So why did you knock twenty-six times? You couldn't have meant "Z" because that doesn't make sense.

Cyr: Number hard.

Me: You find numbers hard?

Cyr: Irevrt here.

Me: Do you mean numbers are irrelevant where you are?

Cyr: Mayb.

Me: Where are you?

Cyr: Void. No place.

Me: Like outer space?

Cyr: No.

Me: Like another dimension?

Cyr: No demtion. Nothing.

Me: Have you been around forever?

Cyr: (Two knocks)

Me: Were you born?

I swear I heard a laugh at this point, but it might have been coming from outside.

Cyr: (Two knocks)

Me: How did you come into existence?

Cyr: Don't now.

Me: Do you have parents?

Cyr: No.

Me: If your answer is yes or no, just knock. It's faster.

Cyr: Time.

Me: Yes, it will save *time*. Do you have any siblings?

Cyr: Man brothers.

Me: You have brothers?

Cyr: (One knock)

Me: Where are they?

Cyr: Here.

Me: What are you exactly?

Cyr: Noting.

Me: Nothing? Is that what you meant to say?

Cyr: (One knock)

Me: Do you have a body?

Cyr: No here.

Me: You don't have a body there?

Cyr: (One knock)

Me: The strange people I'm seeing. Who are they?

Cyr: I.

Me: You? They're *you*?

Cyr: Some.

Me: The little boy and girl.

Cyr: I.

Me: They were you?

Cyr: (One knock)

Me: What about the scary old lady I saw in the window?

Cyr: I.

Me: What about the guys that were staring at me and coming to the house. Was that you?

Cyr: (Two knocks)

Me: Then who were they?

Cyr: Catle.

Me: Like cows?

Cyr: Wortles.

Me: What does that mean? (It took me a moment) They're "worthless"?

Cyr: (One knock)

Me: Why were they coming to my house when I don't even know them?

Cyr: Draw.

Me: Draw? You want me to draw something?

Cyr: (Two knocks)

Cyr: Drawn.

Me: You mean they were drawn here?

Cyr: (One knock)

Me: Why were they drawn here?

Cyr: I.

Me: Because of you?

Cyr: (One knock)

Me: Will there be any more of them?

Cyr: (Two knocks)

Me: That's good. Are you the devil?

Cyr: (Two knocks)

Me: Do you know who the devil is?

Cyr: (One knock)

Me: Do you want to hurt me?

Cyr: Sometime.

Me: Why?

Cyr: Angre

Me: Why are you angry with me?

Cyr: Not u

Me: You're not angry with me?

Cyr: Sometime.

Me: You're talking in circles, Cyr.

Cyr: Sory.

Hey! I made a demon apologize! Lol.

Me: So if you were haunting me and Blythe, are you haunting other people too?

Cyr: (One knock)

Me: How many?

Cyr: Many

Me: You can't count?

Cyr: (two knocks)

Me: Is it more than ten?

Cyr: (One knock)

Me: Is it more than a hundred?

Cyr: (One knock)

Me: Is it more than a million?

Cyr: (One knock)

Me: Is it more than a billion?

Cyr: (Two knocks)

Me: So it's over a million, but under a billion. So you can count a little then?

Cyr: (One knock)

Me: What do you eat?

Cyr: Peple

Me: You eat people?

Cyr: (One knock)

Me: How?

Cyr: Don't know.

Me: That murder that the police kept asking me about – did you have anything to do with that?

Cyr: No.

Me: What exactly do you want from me?

Cyr: All

Me: What does that mean? You want all of me?

Cyr: (One knock)

Me: Well you can't have me, Cyr. You can't have "all" of me, you can't have *any* of me.

Cyr: Already have.

Me: You already have me?

Cyr: (One knock)

Me: How do you have me?

Cyr: Eat.

Me: You're eating me?

Cyr: (One knock)

Me: You're not eating me, Cyr. I'm right here and there are no bite marks in me.

Cyr: No teeth.

Me: You don't have teeth?

Cyr: (Two knocks)

Cyr: Scrath

Me: Do you mean "scratch"? Did you scratch me, Cyr?

Cyr: (One knock)

Me: That wasn't very nice.

Cyr: Sry.

At this point I was getting tired. It might not seem like that long of a conversation, but it was. We took several breaks. Sometimes he'd stop answering for an hour or so before starting up again. Sometimes he'd knock so slowly that it took forever to get an answer. Sometimes he wouldn't leave a long enough break between letters so I couldn't tell when one letter ended and another began, so he'd have to repeat the whole thing.

Like I said, it was very frustrating. But I think I gained some insight into him and what he wants. If I can get to know him, I can figure out how to get rid of him. Plus, I have a written log of a conversation with a non-human entity. Am I the first person to have done that? I'm not sure. Maybe I can get rich and famous from this!

Right at the end of this conversation, I asked if he could promise to leave me alone for at least twelve hours so I could get some good sleep. He said yes and he kept his promise. I'll try talking to him again tomorrow. I'm not sure it's a "him," but that's how I'm going to refer to him.

LAURA'S STORY

Laura is another person I found online and started talking to. She told me her story. I ended up calling the police in Indianapolis (where she's from). I'll think you'll understand why in a moment.

Laura told me she thinks she's a vampire. Intriguing, right? Someone tells you they're a vampire, makes you want to inquire further. We started chatting and she said it all started when she went to the bar for her friend's 21st birthday. She got really drunk and was talking to some guy. Her friends wanted to leave and go to a different bar, but Laura was having a good time with this guy, Peter, who she described as "super hot." She said he would have been perfect if he was taller. Not a super-important part of the story, but an interesting detail.

Her friends left and she stayed behind with Peter. They ended up leaving together. She would have invited him back to her place, but she was living with her mom and two sisters. Peter had a bunch of roommates and shared a room with one, so he wouldn't be comfortable having her over. They ended up getting a hotel room. She told her mom she'd be crashing at her friends' so nobody was expecting her home.

I'll spare you the graphic details of what Laura and Peter did at the hotel. (She sure didn't spare them with me). But she said she woke up in the morning and there was no sign of him. She was also really sore. She said her whole body hurt. There wasn't a mark on her, but she just hurt everywhere. Kind of like when you're stiff the day after going to the gym, but worse.

She got home and talked to her friends. This is where it gets weird. She apologized for not leaving with her friends and staying behind with some guy. Her friends didn't know what she was talking about. They said they never saw her with any guy. They said she was sitting by herself and just didn't want to go with them. Laura was confused but thought maybe they just didn't remember because they were drunk.

Laura said the soreness in her body went away throughout the day but she started to get really thirsty. She drank a tonne of water but it didn't help.

Over the next few days she began losing weight without an explanation. She was eating like normal. Her skin also started to turn an ugly colour. Like a pale white. She said she started looking older too. Her mom and sisters started asking about it. She was worried that Peter gave her some sort of disease.

She went to the doctor and they ran a bunch of tests on her but found nothing wrong.

Laura says her thirst continued, but it wasn't a thirst for water. It was a thirst for blood. She'd never drank blood before but she couldn't shake the thought that doing so would make her feel so much better.

A couple of days later, when she couldn't bear it anymore, she cut her finger and tried drinking it. It didn't quench her thirst. Then she realized it had to be *someone else's* blood.

Her thirst got so bad she snuck into her sister's room one night and cut her arm while she slept and drank the blood that leaked out. After drinking it, she ran to the bathroom and puked.

Her sister woke up soon after with a gash on her arm and blood all over her sheets. The other sister was away for the weekend so it didn't take long for Laura to be accused. She finally admitted she did it but she couldn't say why.

Her mom was sick of how weird she was acting lately and assumed she was on drugs, so she kicked Laura out of the house.

Laura moved into a cheap apartment that her mom helped pay the first month's rent for. She said she felt like she *was* a drug addict, going through heroin withdrawal. It was awful. She curled up on the ground and thought about drinking blood.

Finally, she went out "hunting." That's what she called it. She walked around in the middle of the night until she found some sketchy-looking guy and asked if he could give her a ride. He did and she stabbed him to death and spent the next hour drinking his blood.

Now I don't know how much, if any, of this story is true, but if it is, I can't just *not* report a murder. I already had legal trouble of my own. If the police down there bust her and search her phone, they'll see our conversation and know I knew about it and did nothing. They might call the Edmonton police and have me arrested for being an accessory or something.

So I called the Indianapolis police and reported it. I emailed them screenshots of our conversation then I blocked Laura. That was a week ago and I haven't heard anything about, so maybe it was all Laura's stupid fantasy. But I thought it was interesting enough to share with you guys.

Oh, yeah, it's New Year's Eve! I wasn't even paying attention. I was just sitting here typing, when all of a sudden, I heard fireworks and looked out my window. They were going off at the Ledge Grounds on the other side of the river, downtown. I can see them from my window, which is pretty cool. It's kind of strange to be sitting home alone while everyone else is out there, getting drunk and partying. Hopefully this isn't a sign of things to come. Hopefully by next New Year's things will be back to normal.

Happy New Year's, everyone! Have a drink on me!

WEDNESDAY, JANUARY 1, 2020

I feel better now that I can talk with this demon. It's like I have some control. Communication is progress. Ignoring him was getting nowhere. Maybe I can reason with him. He did keep his promise about letting me sleep without doing anything to me, so at least I know he's not *all* bad.

I'm talking with Cyr again, using the same method as Monday night. He's communicating better, but it's still a long process. I'm making notes again and I'll type them up tomorrow. In case you're wondering, my notebook is full of short-hand notes with questions and tick-marks as I count his knocks and write the corresponding letter of the alphabet.

Hard to believe it's the 2020s! The roaring 20s! I think the 1920s were much cooler than the 2020s, but what are you gonna do?

THURSDAY, JANUARY 2, 2020

The sun has risen and, once again, I spent the whole night talking to a demon. I was going to type up my notes after I slept, but I drank too much coffee and now I'm wired and can't sleep.

This time the conversation ended when he stopped talking. I guess my demon doesn't have good manners. At least I got him to promise to leave me alone again when I go to sleep.

Here's the conversation:

Me: What is your gender?

Cyr: Many.

Me: Do you mean "man"?

Cyr: (Two knocks)

Me: You mean many?

Cyr: (One knock)

Me: You're many genders?

Cyr: (Two knocks)

Me: You're one of many people?

Cyr: (Two knocks)

Me: Right, you're not a "person." You're one of many demons?

Cyr: (Two knocks)

Me: I mean, you're one of many "entities" or whatever the hell you are?

Cyr: (One knock)

Me: So you don't have a gender?

Cyr: (Two knocks)

Me: Ok.

Cyr: Pop.

Me: Pop? What does that mean?

Cyr: Having fun.

Me: You're having fun?

Cyr: (One knock)

Me: Good. But give me sensical answers so you don't confuse me. Do you hate me?

Cyr: Once.

Me: You hated me once?

There was no answer.

Me: Just answer with knocks. Do you hate me?

Cyr: (One knock)

Me: So you hate me. That's not very nice, Cyr.

Cyr: Way I am.

Me: Why do you hate me?

Cyr: Insignificant.

I should note that this is the most complicated answer it's given yet and it spelled it correctly.

Me: To continue with a question from yesterday, when you say you're "eating" me, do you mean you're draining my energy?

Cyr: (One knock)

Me: Wow. I can't believe that's true.

On a side note, I think this is a really big revelation. I've been reading lots about this concept and up until now it's just been a theory.

Me: Is there a God?

Cyr: I am God.

Me: You're not God, Cyr. God is good.

Cyr: (Two knocks)

Cyr: I more powerful.

Me: I think you're conceited.

Cyr: I think so I God.

Me: I don't think it works like that, Cyr. *I* think. Does that mean *I'm* God?

Cyr: No.

Me: Why not?

Cyr: I power you shit.

Cyr swore at me!

Me: Cyr! That's not nice!

Cyr: Sory.

Me: You didn't want to answer this question last time, but it's really important, so please answer it. How did Blythe die?

Cyr: Death.

Me: She died by death? Thanks, Cyr. That really helps.

Cyr: Sacrastc.

Me: Yes, I was being sarcastic! Tell me how Blythe died.

Cyr: Kill

Me: She was killed?

Cyr: Scare.

Me: She died from being scared?

Cyr: (One knock)

Me: Was it you who scared her?

Cyr: (One knock)

Me: Then technically you killed her.

Cyr: (Two knocks)

Me: Maybe you're not under the same legal jurisdiction as us, but if you scare someone to death, you're at least partly to blame.

Cyr: Her fault.

Me: It was *her* fault you scared her to death?

Cyr: Her fault I exit.

Me: Her fault you "exit"?

Cyr: Exist.

Me: How is it her fault you exist?

Cyr: Believe.

Me: She believed in you?

Cyr: (One knock)

Me: Not that I don't love having you around, but how do I get rid of you?

Cyr: Don't.

Me: I'm not giving you a choice, Cyr. How do I get rid of you?

Cyr: Later.

Me: Tell me now.

Cyr: (Two knocks)

Me: Cyr…tell me now.

Cyr: Other day.

Me: You'll tell me another day?

Cyr: (One knock)

Me: Promise?

Cyr: (One knock)

Me: Can we talk again tomorrow?

There was no answer. But at least I got him open to the idea of telling me how to get rid of him. Of course, I'm sure he'll want something in return. I can't just expect him to tell me how to vanquish him. What's *he* get out of it? I'm willing to do anything. At least the lines of communication are open now.

I'm starting to think it's kind of cool that I have this thing. It's like my own personal ghost. Who knows what kind of stuff he can tell me? Maybe there's a way I can make money off it. Like holding seances or something. They'll be real, not stupid and fake like that one Blythe took me to.

Anyways, I'm so beyond tired right now. I'm going to bed.

THURSDAY, JANUARY 2, 2020

I had a good sleep. Again. Sleep is so underrated.

I got an email from Blythe's sister today. I don't know how she got my email address. Probably off Blythe's phone. She said Blythe died of heart failure. That's interesting. Heart failure from fear, maybe? She said they're not having a funeral; they're just having a small family gathering. She didn't invite me and I didn't ask. I was *Blythe's* friend. I don't give a fuck about her family.

Oh, my God, I received an email from some weird address that had a video attached. Normally I wouldn't have clicked on it because it could be a virus, but the subject line said, "Message from Dad." So I clicked on it and watched it. Sure enough it was a video of my dad. Or at least something that looked like my dad. My dad's long dead in case you forgot. In the video, he was sitting in the living room of some really nice house I've never seen before. This is what he said:

Hey, Genesis, how's my little girl? It's been a while. I've missed you a lot. I think about you all the time. I hope you're doing good in school. I'd really like to see you again. If you want, maybe we could meet for coffee or something. If you're not too busy, maybe we could go fishing in the mountains again. I don't know where you're living now, but I could come see you. I love you.

Logic dictates it's not really my dad. I went to his funeral. If he somehow faked his death and now wants to come back into my life, he would have addressed his "death." So I'm assuming it's my friendly neighbourhood demon fucking with me. I replied to the email and said, "Fuck you, Cyr." The second I hit send there was a loud pound on the wall.

This is so weird. I guess demons have gone digital. It reminds me of what happened with Joel and him getting the threatening texts. If he can do this, what else can he do? It has me thinking he emailed something to that Erin woman from the clothing store and that's why she was so mad at me. That's kind of freaky to think about. What if he starts posting stuff on my social media accounts?

I forward the video to my mom. Maybe that will get her attention.

Another thing I've been thinking about – Cyr doesn't seem that smart. Aren't demons in movies usually intelligent? In Exorcist, it was. They can speak eloquently and seem to know a lot of shit. Cyr is either really stupid or really young. And our "conversations" are so long and frustrating. I have to talk to him again to find out how to get rid of him, and I'm definitely not looking forward to it. I have to talk to him for eight hours or more just to have what would be a two-minute conversation with a normal person. This whole knocking thing is so tedious it's almost not worth it. I'm pretty sure I've heard him speak out loud before. I wish I could talk to him face-to-face. Although I might regret saying that if I ever saw his actual form. I guess he doesn't have enough energy to speak out loud very often. Maybe he needs to scare me more to talk and take human form. I'd love to hear a scientist's take on this. What kind of organism feeds on negative emotions? That makes sense in science fiction or horror movies, not real life.

JOSH'S STORY

Since we're on the topic of ghosts and computers, I thought I'd tell you about another one of my interesting internet pen pals. I was talking with this guy named Josh from Australia. He told me he thought his house was haunted. He never saw anything scary but one day, out of the blue, he was just *scared*. He said it was the middle of the afternoon and nothing was out of the ordinary. He was sitting there and all of a sudden, he got that feeling when your hair stands on end. He said he was scared for no reason. Like there was something in his house, coming for him. He couldn't explain it, but the feeling didn't go away. He ended up leaving the house until he felt better. He came home and the second he walked through the door, it hit him again. The fear. Like me, he didn't have anywhere to go, so he was forced to just deal with it. He said no matter where in his house he was or what he was doing, he was just scared out of his mind.

This went on for a couple days, then he started noticing his friends on social media acting weird. They'd send him strange PMs and make bizarre comments on his posts. At first it was one person and he thought maybe their account had been hacked. But then more people started acting weird and after a few days it was everybody.

He said by the end, every one of his friends was messaging him multiple times per day with weird gibberish and threats. And this happened on all his platforms. He ended up cancelling all his social media accounts.

This happened while he and I were conversing. I wondered what happened because he just vanished one day. He resurfaced a few days later, contacting me on email. He said email was the only method of communication where he wasn't being harassed. We talked on email for a while, but then he stopped replying. That was a couple weeks ago, so who knows what happened.

Haunting in a digital age….

This is fucked up! It's bad. Really bad. I took a nap and I felt something jump on my bed and start choking me! I couldn't see it, but I could feel its fingers around my neck. I thought I was going to die, then it suddenly stopped. I jumped up to run out of the room but the door slammed shut and something pushed me down. I hit my head on the doorknob. I got up and ran out of the room. I tried to run for my front door but it pushed me down again and dragged me down the hall by my hair, into the living room.

I could hear it growling. It finally let go and I ran out of my apartment. I was freaking out, practically in tears in the elevator. People got in on the way down. They asked if I was ok and I didn't answer. What am I supposed to say? When the elevator got to the lobby, I pushed them out of the way and ran out of the building.

I know it was Cyr. That fucking asshole said he'd leave me alone, then attacks me.

I'm sitting on a bench in a park near my house. I don't know what I'm supposed to do now.

Ok, now I'm in a church. I started walking around and Cyr followed me! He kept pushing me on the street and slapping me. It's just after 11:00pm and I saw a church with lights on and some cars in the parking lot. Not the church across from my house. This one's way down in another neighbourhood. The doors were unlocked and I went inside. I couldn't see anyone here, but there's a lot of laughing and yelling and coming from the basement. And singing. I think there's some sort of youth group going on. I'm hiding out in the main area (not sure what it's called) with the pews and pulpit and all that.

Cyr hasn't touched me since I came in. Maybe he can't enter because it's a church. I'm going to hide out here until they kick me out. Or maybe I'll be lucky and they won't see me and I can spend the night.

But what do I do after that?

FRIDAY, JANUARY 3, 2020

It's morning. I'm still at the church, writing this on my phone. Those people in the basement left around 1:00am last night. They locked up but didn't see me.

I walked around the church for a while, checking it out. It's pretty big. I don't know what kind of a church this is. I didn't bother to look. I just ran inside. Luckily, they didn't have an alarm or I'd be spending the night in jail. Or on the street. Both of which I'd prefer to my own apartment at this point.

Years ago I would have found a dark church in the middle of the night scary as fuck. But now it actually seems peaceful. I found a Bible and read some of it. There was mention of demons and I couldn't help wondering if any of them was Cyr. Probably not, but you never know.

I found a couch in one of the rooms and tried to sleep but couldn't. I might have dozed off for a bit, but not much. In the morning, I heard someone coming and peaked out the door. There was a lady going around turning on lights. She almost saw me, but I managed to get out without being seen.

Now I'm sitting on that same bench I was yesterday, near my apartment. I can see my building from here. And I'm terrified of it. I'm seriously thinking of never going back. Maybe I can just be a street person. There's lots of homeless people in the city and they all manage somehow. Is that a preferable life to being attacked by an invisible entity? I'm not sure.

I'm sitting here, wondering when he's going to attack me again. What if he pushes me in front of a bus?!

So I guess it's official. Cyr can't be trusted after all! Blythe was right. He's a fucking liar. I can't believe I was thinking about being friends with him.

The religion thing might work. It really hated that priest. And it didn't follow me into the church. It said it wasn't scared of the priest, but maybe it was lying so I wouldn't bring one back.

Maybe if I give it an ultimatum, I can get it to leave! Now I'm all fired up! I'm actually typing this as I walk back to my apartment. I'm not going to let him scare me. That's what he *wants*. He needs me to be afraid to survive. So really, I hold the power here. If I'm not afraid, he's weak. I'm in fucking control, Cyr! Not you!

I got home and nothing happened. I never locked my door when I ran out so I'm glad I wasn't robbed. I've been home for an hour and he hasn't touched me or done anything. I've been calling out for him with no response. No way I'm naïve enough to think he's actually gone. We're long past that now. It's just a matter of time before he makes his presence known.

Cyr, you childish, stupid demon! You don't scare me!

It's evening and still no "word" from Cyr. But I did get a reply from my mom. She freaked out at me for that video of my dad. She called me the "C" word. (I'm incapable of actually writing or saying that word). She accused me of faking the video. Yeah, Mom, I made a perfect recreation of Dad using my amazingly advanced makeup skills.

I didn't even read her full rant. She was just yelling, calling me a bad daughter, saying she never should have had me. Whatever. That might have bothered me in the past, but it means nothing now. Fuck her. I deleted the message. Not even worth responding to.

I finally got a hold of Cyr. I think the little bastard is afraid of me. I kept knocking and calling out to him. He finally started knocking back. This is the conversation we just had:

Me: Listen up, Cyr! I've had enough of your shit! You leave now or I'm calling another priest to come over and bless the house. I'm going to do that every single day until you leave! (Two powerful knocks)

You don't want me to call a priest? (Two knocks)

Then get out and never come back! (Two knocks)

You can't have it both ways. I know you hate the religious stuff, so I'm going to use it to torture you! Maybe I'll sing a song about Jesus! (Two knocks)

I started singing this stupid, catchy religious song I heard in a stoner movie called "Hot Box."

Jesus was a little lamb

Who spread his word throughout the land

He had a robe and he had a beard

And a father in Heaven whom Satan feared.

While I was singing, I could feel this tension in the room, like something building up. The kitchen drawer opened and my bedroom door slammed. Then I heard this voice yell, "Stop!" and suddenly the tension released. I guess I really pissed Cyr off. So I continued taunting him:

Me: I'm going to keep singing! And I'm calling a priest unless you leave!

There was no answer.

Me: What's the matter? You afraid now?! Where's the big man that was pushing me around?!

Still no answer. Maybe he used all his energy shouting, "No!" The funny thing is, for the first time, when he said, "No!" I heard *fear* in his voice. That's reassuring. If I can keep the pressure on him, I can get rid of him.

Tomorrow I'll call a priest again. I might have to try a different religion. They might be hesitant after the last priest they sent vanished.

I didn't hear from Cyr for the next few hours, but when I was using my phone, it kept fucking up. It would turn off or restart at random. Apps wouldn't load. It was really annoying. Not sure if it's my phone being shitty or Cyr fucking with my electronic devices.

So this is where we're at. I think I'm winning the fight. I got him scared. If he hates the religion, I'll sing religious songs all fucking day. I'll hold prayer circles or bible studies here. Whatever I have to do to drive him out.

I wonder where Dan is and what he's doing.

Cyr resurfaced. He started knocking and I knocked back. He learns the more we talk. The first time it was like talking to a 2-year-old, the next time a 5-year-old. Now he was like a teenager. He could actually talk (or "knock") in full sentences. We did the whole one knock is "A," two is "B," etc. Here's the conversation:

Me: You want to talk? (One knock)

Are you going to be nice and do as I say? (One knock)

Side note: It's like dealing with a child. You have to be firm or they'll walk all over you.

Me: Here's the way it's gonna be. I want you gone. Is there a way to make that happen? (A long pause, then one knock)

Me: How?

Cyr: Pass me to someone.

Me: I have to pass you on to somebody else? (One knock)

Me: Like Blythe did to me? (One knock)

Me: Who?

Cyr: Who what?

Me: Who do I have to pass you on to?

Cyr: Anyon.

Me: If I pass you on to somebody else, you'll leave me alone forever? (One knock)

Me: How do I know you're not lying?

Cyr: I have no reason to lei. Matter not who I get energy from. You not special.

It took half an hour to get that answer out of him. Long breaks between letters and words.

Me: So what do I have to do?

Cyr: You now.

Me: Are you trying to say, "You *know*"? (One knock)

Me: I have to get somebody's hair, burn it, wrap it around twigs, then recite that shit Blythe told me and leave the object in somebody's home. Is that correct?

Cyr: No burn.

Me: I don't have to burn the hair? (Two knocks)

Me: But otherwise, what I just said is correct? (One knock)

This was pretty much the end of the conversation. He's getting smarter and better at communicating.

There's an end in sight. A real end. For some reason, I trust him on this. He's right – why would he care who he gets his "energy" from? Humans are all the same to him.

But who am I going to pass it on to? Whose hair can I get? I don't have any living friends and I'm not currently associating with any members of the human race. And it can't just be someone off the street. I have to be able to get into their home. So strangers are out of the question.

It just came to me! Mrs. Pearson! She's been pissing me off anyways. This afternoon, she approached me outside the building. She said she's been seeing people come to my apartment and hearing strange noises inside. She's worried about me. I told her to fuck off. Who I have over and what goes on in my apartment is none of her business. She said, "You used to be such a nice girl," and walked away.

Who is she talking about? There hasn't been anyone strange coming to my apartment since those guys stopped showing up. As far as I know. Maybe they're coming without my knowledge, but I haven't seen any of them and there hasn't been any non-Cyr knocking on my door. So I think Mrs. Pearson is full of shit.

Either way, she's my best bet for passing the demon to. I wouldn't feel bad about it. But there's still the matter of getting her hair and getting in and out of her apartment without detection. This might take some thinking.

As I was typing that last part, I felt a presence in my room and something touching my hair. I said, "Cyr! Leave me alone or I'll start singing again!" Instantly, the touching stopped and the presence was gone. My bedroom door slammed closed from the suction as it left.

It's 2:00am. I just worked up the nerve to try Mrs. Pearson's apartment. There was an outside chance she doesn't lock her door at night. But I checked. And she does. So I need to find another way to get in and get her hair. I can't follow her to the hair salon. Who knows when she'll get her hair cut next? I don't want to wait that long. Doing it while she sleeps is the logical solution. But it means breaking into her apartment, which means I'll need her key.

I just heard a voice whisper, "Die." In Blythe's honour, I said, "So lame, Cyr! You're such a loser." Then I sang that song again and I swear I heard a whimper. Poor baby Cyr was trying not to cry. I think he wants to be passed along as much as I want him to be.

SATURDAY, JANUARY 4, 2020

I am now in possession of Mrs. Pearson's apartment keys! I looked out my window today and saw her unloading groceries from her car, so I ran down and pretended I just happened to be walking by and offered to help. I "apologized" for being a jerk yesterday. When we were dropping the groceries in her apartment, I snagged her keys from her purse.

She came over later and asked if I'd seen them. I said I hadn't. I don't think she believed me, but who gives a fuck?

Tonight, I'm going to sneak into her place and snag some of her hair while she's sleeping. If I get caught, so what? What can they really do? The punishment for trespassing can't be that severe. I'm so eager to end this, nothing scares me anymore.

I guess this precludes me from publishing this book. It might be considered a confession. That would be ironic – my journal that was meant to help me through a difficult time is used in court as evidence against me. Maybe I can wait until Mrs. Pearson dies, then go public. Lol. She's pretty old.

Or I can have some legal statement at the beginning about how the book is "purely a work of fiction," and deny this really happened. So if I *do* publish this book, I'm trusting you guys not to rat on me!

Oh, my God, I just did it! I used the key to sneak into Mrs. Pearson's apartment. First, I went outside and looked up at the building to make sure the lights were out in her apartment, then I went for it. My heart was beating a mile a minute. As soon as I got in, I could hear her snoring, which was a huge relief. I was worried I'd open the door and she'd be standing there and scream and call the cops. I guess luck is on my side.

It was a strange feeling being in somebody's house without them knowing. A bizarre combination of fear and exhilaration. I hope that doesn't make me sound like a psycho. This isn't something I plan to make a habit of.

Her bedroom door was closed so I stood there for a bit to make sure she was definitely asleep (and to work up the nerve). Then I slowly turned her doorknob and entered the room. It was dark, but our building is on a main street so there's lots of light coming in. I could see her lying in bed, face down. As I walked to her bed, I bumped some trunk she had on her floor with my foot and I thought I'd woken her because she stopped snoring. I stood there, frozen for a few moments and eventually her deep breathing resumed and she started snoring again.

For some reason, her snoring angered me and reaffirmed I was doing the right thing. Since we're on the topic of confession, I'll admit the thought of smothering her with a pillow entered my mind. But only briefly. I'd never actually do that. Is it just me, or have I become a super bitch lately? I don't feel bad. I was driven to it.

I approached the bed and snipped off a piece of her hair with scissors. As soon as I did, I could feel Cyr's presence in the room. But I didn't stick around. I ran out of the apartment. I left her door unlocked because I needed to come back.

This afternoon, I grabbed some twigs from the dog-walking park next to the building. I used electrical tape to tape them into a triangle, then taped the hair to it. How this is supposed to pass a demon from one person to another is a mystery to me, but I'm not going to question it. I guess all religions have weird rituals and artifacts for various purposes. *It's not the object, it's the intent.*

I took the object back to Mrs. Pearson's apartment and went into her walk-in storage. That's where Blythe left mine, so it's a logical choice. I said the words Blythe told me, (I'm not repeating them here because I don't want anyone else doing this) and left the object behind some boxes in the corner.

I locked her door when I left, then went outside and dropped her key on the ground next to her parking space. Maybe she'll find it and think she dropped it. Either way, looks like I got away with it. Mrs. Pearson is in for a big surprise!

I'm home now, lying on the couch and everything is calm. For some reason, I'm super tired. Doing that sucked the energy out of me. I don't feel scared at all. I'm going to sleep. I'll guess I'll find out over the coming days if it worked or not.

SUNDAY, JANUARY 5, 2020

I slept like a baby. No scary stuff. Nothing so far today. I tried knocking on the walls and didn't get a response. I sang a Jesus song and nothing happened. Maybe he's really gone. It feels "lighter" in the apartment. I know, I know, I've said that before, but it's different this time. It's like I've woken up from a bad dream.

I'm still prepared for the realization that it's not over and Cyr was lying, but for the first time, I have hope that this is the end. I'll guess we'll see soon.

ELLE'S STORY

For the last "other person's story," I thought I'd use a positive story, just to show that there's always hope. Elle made a post about having undergone an exorcism. It was a paranormal page so obviously people took notice. But I was surprised by how cruel the comments to her were. Especially since she was a 14-year-old girl. I sent her a PM and we messaged back and forth. She said scary stuff started happening in her house, but only to her. Not her brother or parents. She told her parents what was happening but they didn't believe her. Only her brother did. Not because he witnessed anything, but because he just believed her (i.e. he wasn't an asshole). Her brother was 12.

An aggravating factor was that their dad physically abused both of them. I would have called the police to report it but both her parents died.

Elle said the scary stuff started with noises, then turned into voices, then moving objects, then pushing and pinching her (sound familiar?). One time, the "ghost man," as she called it, left a big bruise on her arm. A teacher at school called social services and the police went to the house to speak to Elle's dad. Lucky for him, he was away for the previous few days, so couldn't be responsible. Elle's brother took the blame for it so his sister didn't have to tell the police the truth. They couldn't arrest a 12-year-old so that was the end of that.

But Elle's dad freaked out and beat his wife, assuming the marks came from another man who'd been in the house while he was away.

Elle said after that incident, she began acting "weird." Her brother and parents would tell her she did stuff she had no recollection of. One day she was grounded because she "hurt daddy." She had no idea what she did.

She researched online and joined paranormal groups on social media. She began to think she was possessed. She told her brother and made him promise not to tell their parents. She wanted to get an exorcism. Together, they went to a church. I asked if it was Catholic church and she didn't know. She just said they went to the closest church to their house. They talked to a "church guy" but he said he couldn't help. He wanted to talk to their parents, so they ran out.

Soon after, both their parents died in separate incidents. Their dad had a heart attack and their mom died of a stroke within days of each other.

Elle's new personality began acting out even more and her brother was scared. They watched YouTube videos on how to do an exorcism and her little brother performed it himself (how cute). She claimed it worked and she's back to normal now and happy.

Her and her brother are living with their aunt and everything is fine. I have the feeling she wasn't really possessed. She was likely acting out because of her terrible home life. But I'm glad the story has a happy ending.

TUESDAY, JANUARY 10, 2020

It's been almost a week and everything has been perfectly calm in my apartment. No paranormal stuff. No *maybe*-paranormal stuff. Life as usual. Looks like Cyr's gone for good!

I've stopped drinking and taking the sleeping pills to fall asleep. I've been sleeping well.

I left the apartment last night to run to the store and as I passed Mrs. Pearson's apartment, I heard banging coming from inside. Like someone pounding on the walls. Oh, well. Better her than me. I don't want to seem cruel, I'm just glad it's over. You have no idea how good I feel. I can finally get on with my life.

I found a new apartment! It's a one-bedroom in Capilano. It's a little cheaper than this place. I'm moving in at the end of the month. (I sold a bunch more stuff to get money for the damage deposit.) I'm looking forward to leaving this place behind. And I have another job interview on Thursday! It's with a shipping company. Now that Cyr (and the police) are off my back, I'm sure it will go just fine.

I'm cutting ties with everyone who was part of this nightmare - Dan, my mom, Melinda, Mike, Addilyn. Basically anyone in my life. I'm starting fresh. 2020 will be my year!

I decided to go ahead and actually publish this book! So it looks like people will be reading it after all! So thank you! Yes, *you*. The person reading this right now. You're awesome! I think I might publish it under a pseudonym so it looks like it's a work of fiction. So I don't get in trouble for the illegal stuff I did. Lol.

Anyways, I could write more, but who wants to hear about my day-to-day life? lol. Maybe if something fascinating happens, I'll start another journal. But until then, thanks for going on this journey with me! I hope to meet you one day!

SATURDAY, FEBRUARY 15, 2020

Hi! It's me again! Just a little epilogue. I'm getting close to publishing the book! I got the artwork done and everything.

I got that job and it's great! My new apartment is awesome. No scary stuff.

But something worth noting happened. I drove past my old building and saw Ghost Girl scampering around outside. And there was an old lady with her. Yeah, you guessed it. The same old lady I saw floating outside my window. It nearly stopped my heart. The old lady saw me and followed me with her eyes.

I just can't help but worry that Cyr is out there. Looking for me. Biding his time.

THE END

About the Author

Brandon Rhiness is an author, screenwriter and filmmaker based in Edmonton, Alberta, Canada. He wrote the screenplays for such films as John, 316 and Cor Values. He wrote and directed the films Hot Box and Cold Comfort.

Brandon also writes comic books and has published many under his company, Higher Universe Comics.

I'm Haunted is Brandon's first novel. He hopes it's the first of many!

Contact Brandon

Facebook: https://www.facebook.com/brandonrhinesswriter

Twitter: @brandonrhiness

Instagram: @brandonrhiness

Email: rhiness@thehigheruniverse.com